*COWBOY*

**Jerry Raine**

Copyright © 2015 by Jerry Raine.

This novel is a work of fiction. Names, characters, places and incidents are either the product of the author's imagination, or, if real, used fictitiously.

For Sabrina and Jemima.

And to the memory of old school friend Tony Skinner.

'I need one guitar to play when I'm down, and one bed to sleep on when I'm tired, I need one CD when I wanna hear some sound, and one bottle of wine when I need to be inspired.'

## *CHAPTER ONE.*

As he walked towards his local tube station on a summer's afternoon, the last person Jason Campbell expected to see coming towards him was a famous film star. She was walking very slowly, lost in her dreamy world, but when she noticed he was carrying a guitar she looked right at him and almost smiled. Jason tried to smile as well but was too nervous, and then the moment was gone; the film star was past him and heading off to God knows where, while he was heading into the station.

Jason almost stopped in his tracks. He wanted to turn around and look at her, make sure he wasn't seeing things. Could that really be her? But he knew her face very well from various movies over the years, and he knew that she acted in a British TV series called *Prince and Langer* about two female cops in London. He just didn't know that she lived in this particular part of town. Or maybe she was just visiting, coming to see a friend for the day.

With a racing heart Jason went through the ticket barriers and up the stairs to the platform. He stood waiting for his District Line train wondering if he'd really just seen the American actress Sara Shriver. Why on earth would she be in Chiswick, west London? He would have to look her up on the Internet when he got home, see if she lived in the area. He cursed the fact that he didn't have a smart phone so he could just look her up right now on the train journey to Islington.

Instead he took out his cheap mobile, bought in Virgin for £10, and sent a text to his film buff friend Arty who lived near Maidstone in Kent: *I just saw Sara Shriver walking down the street. Am I excited or what!*

It didn't take long for Arty to reply. Probably two minutes. His text said: *Forget her. She's out of your league. She once had an affair with Burt Reynolds.*

Jason felt his spirits nosedive. An affair with Burt Reynolds? What a let down. Then he remembered the film. It had been made when Sara was quite young, a crime film with several car chases. Sara had been a young woman then, probably in her early twenties or maybe even her late teens and Reynolds must have been in his thirties. Fancy her having an affair with him. It was almost a disgusting thought, though Reynolds had been one of the biggest stars in the world at the time. Jason remembered seeing him in *The Mean Machine* which he'd enjoyed. And the *Smokey and the Bandit* films were fairly entertaining as well. Sara Shriver must now be in her late forties or early fifties. Jason would find that out later too.

He texted Arty back: *Thanks for that. You've just soiled her in my mind. Now I'll keep my hands off her.*

Arty texted back a smiley face, done with a colon and half a bracket.

Still in a daze Jason stared out of the window at the passing scenery. He liked living in this part of west London and he liked it even more now that he knew that Sara Shriver was living there too. Or was she? He couldn't get her out of his head.

What other films had he seen her in? There was a film called *No Depression*, based on a well known literary novel, where he remembered she'd had a very long topless scene. But what else? He couldn't think of anything, though there must surely be some more. She must have made a big impression on him because he'd always fancied her. He had never seen her TV series *Prince and Langer* though, it just wasn't his type of thing, and it was on ITV, a channel he rarely watched. But maybe now he would try and get it on DVD. Maybe he could find it cheap in a charity shop or on Amazon.

The train left the over ground section of railway and then went underground. Jason took a book from the pouch on his soft guitar case and tried to read but his mind wasn't on it. He tried thinking about the evening ahead, another waste-of-time gig in a small Islington pub with about fifty people present. He was getting paid £20, which after travel and a few beers would see him make a profit of about £5 at the most. Still, it got him out of his flat and meeting people. That was about the only good thing he could say about it. Plus he had just seen Ms Shriver. That was something to brighten up the day for sure.

Jason had been living in Chiswick for about two years and he'd seen a few other famous people walking around. Off the top of his head he could think of several England rugby players, one faded TV actress, plus several TV presenters whose faces he knew but not their names. Chiswick was a wealthy part of London and had some very nice property in the area. He could understand why famous people lived there. And about a decade ago Jason had almost been famous himself of course. He had to smile at that. But those dreams seemed to have faded now for good.

He had sold his house in Woodvale, Surrey just over two years ago, determined to leave suburbia behind and spend the latter part of his life in more exciting surroundings. He was now over fifty and heading for old age, still single, but determined to go out on a high. But when he'd bought his flat in Chiswick, the mortgage and bills were so steep that he'd found he had little time or money for socialising at all, so he was in effect a prisoner inside his own home. He was working so hard, taking on more and more guitar lessons, that he barely had time to do anything else, just get out of the house one or two evenings a week to play some live music in some grotty pub in another part of London. His life was music, music and more music, and nothing else. But isn't that what he'd always wanted?

Back in Woodvale he had almost hit the big time some eleven or so years ago. He'd had one CD out on an American independent label called *The Quiet One*, and although the reviews had been good, the sales had been poor and a second one hadn't been forthcoming. Jason had recorded his own CD instead – called *One Guitar* - using just himself and two local musicians for backing, and sold it at gigs that his agent Charles Penn had been getting for him. He always went down well at the concerts – as a support act for visiting American country singers like Tift Merritt and Mindy Smith – and he managed to sell quite a few CDs too. But after a couple of years of good touring Charles Penn had stopped getting him gigs; there were so many singers around that someone else deserved a chance, and Penn couldn't give all the choice gigs to him. So, the concerts had dried up and so had the CD sales. Jason was now resorting to playing £20 gigs – and occasional £50 ones at private parties - anywhere he could find them and selling the occasional CD from his rather basic website. If he ever recorded a third CD he would call it *The Only One to Fall* after one of his newer songs. He liked keeping to the *One* titles - just so people got the point that he was a solitary man living the life of a lonesome picker.

He'd also had one other pleasing success – the sale of one of his songs which had appeared on two country albums over in Nashville. The song was called 'Private Eye' and had been on his first CD. Someone somewhere had heard it and the next thing he knew it had been snapped up for an album by someone called Sheldon Blake. Then a Cajun country guy called Rob Rodriguez had asked for it too and Jason had thought he was on his way. But both of their CDs had sold poorly and Jason hadn't made much money from the song at all, though he still received small cheques for it now and then.

He always lived in hope that one day one of his other songs would be snapped up and recorded by a really big star, or maybe used on a bestselling film soundtrack. He knew the famous story of singer-songwriter Nick Lowe receiving a cheque for a million dollars out of the blue because one of his songs was on the soundtrack to *The Bodyguard*, one of the biggest selling CDs of all time thanks to Whitney Houston being on it. Nick Lowe hadn't even known about it at the time. It was the stroke of luck that could change a life, something that Jason always hoped for but secretly knew would never happen. He was more inclined for bad luck to follow him around. That was just the way things seemed to go, the kind of guy he was destined to be.

Some years ago he had written a song called 'My Life as a Failure'. It was a six minute song that outlined his musical career over the decades, a bit like the classic song 'Rock and Roll I Gave You All the Best Years of My Life'. He rarely performed it live as it was too long, though he knew it was a great song. It wasn't even on either of his CDs. As the years passed by the song took on extra meaning as one disappointment took over from another. His life was basically a downhill spiral of disappointments that he couldn't get out of, though like most people he muddled along well enough. Maybe one day his luck would change, but he wasn't too hopeful.

After several tube changes, Jason arrived in Islington, north London, and began the long walk down Upper Street. His Martin guitar felt heavy slung over his shoulder in its case, and he often wished it was lighter. He had other lighter guitars but the Martin was the most reliable; it had a great acoustic sound and rarely went out of tune on stage. He had bought it for £800 back in the early 1980s, and it was now worth around £2,000. It was his oldest friend, and sometimes he felt paranoid about taking it to gigs in case it got damaged or stolen. It was insured but it would be irreplaceable if it was taken, so Jason often took cheaper guitars instead when he wanted to play. He cursed its weight when he had to make long walks with it though, like this one on Upper Street, a road that seemed to never end.

After fifteen minutes The Hope and Anchor came into view, a pub Jason had played in many times before, first at open mic nights and then later as a headliner. There was a nice guy called Mike who ran the acoustic evenings and a stunning barmaid called Gill who he fancied. She was in her mid-thirties so probably just out of reach age wise, but they got on well and flirted with each other. She had shoulder length wavy red hair and a full body, with a cleavage Jason always found his eyes wandering to.

Gill had picked him up on that once. 'One day your eyes are going to pop out,' she'd told him.

Jason had quickly replied, 'My contact lenses will keep them in,' while feeling his face flush at the same time.

He wondered if there was a finer looking woman in the world. Certainly not in *his* world, though maybe Sara Shriver would push her close.

There was nothing more he would like to see than Gill's breasts, and maybe one day it would happen. Until it did he would have to make do with a lovely photo he'd found of her on Facebook, sitting in a garden somewhere in a low-cut T-shirt vest that beautifully showed off her breasts and plenty of cleavage. He had saved the photo to his laptop and used it as a screensaver. It was one of the perks of being on Facebook, probably the only perk; women often put photos on there that should really only be for private viewing, or they were snapped by other people and then put online without them knowing. Jason was forever grateful to whoever had taken that photo of Gill. If only she knew.

He stepped inside The Hope and Anchor and there she was behind the bar serving someone. She looked up and smiled at him. Jason smiled back at his Hope, glad to get rid of the guitar weight, his Anchor, off his back.

## *CHAPTER TWO.*

Upstairs in The Hope and Anchor games room, two men in their mid-twenties were playing pool, and in between shots, looking out of the window at the women on the street below.

'Jesus! Look at this one,' said the fatter of the two.

He was leaning out and pointing down at the tables on the pavement where people were sitting in the warm summer evening, drinking their pints and breathing in car fumes. His name was Ray Lane and he worked in IT. He was making too much money and had been single most of his life, mainly because he ate and drank too much and was overweight. His friend Jamie came over and leaned out of the window too.

'Jesus indeed,' Jamie said. 'Little does she know the great view we get from up here. I could spit right down on to her cleavage.'

'Yeah,' Ray said, 'then go and rub your dick all over her. Spit and polish.'

Jamie laughed then stopped himself. 'Your mouth. You're fucking disgusting.'

'That's what keeps my world a-turnin',' Ray said, then went back to the pool table and played a pathetic shot. Being overweight Ray wasn't much good at sports; that's if you could call pool a sport. And his back and neck were aching from being out in the sun too long the day before, which made leaning over a pool table a little uncomfortable.

Jamie had laughed when he'd seen his red face, calling him a redneck. Ray had laughed it off, though he didn't care too much for the description.

Jamie left the window and came back for his shot. 'Did you see the barmaid downstairs? She had a rack on her as well.'

'Yeah, beautiful,' Ray said. 'I'd love to get my sweaty little hands on her.'

'Yeah, that will never happen. But we'll have to get back here more often. See if *I* can chat her up.'

'Out of your league,' Ray said. 'The only rack you'll get your hands on is this rack of pool balls.'

They turned around then as someone entered the room, a guy carrying a guitar and a pint.

'Couldn't help but hearing,' said the guy. 'Yes, she's way out of your league.'

He smiled at them both and Jamie wondered if he was taking the piss. 'You know about her then?' he asked.

The man nodded and said, 'Yeah. I've been friends with her a while.'

'Does she have a boyfriend?' Ray asked.

'No,' said the man. 'And I don't think she's looking either.'

'That's a pity,' Jamie said. 'I'd fancy my chances.'

The man didn't say anything, just looked at him with a superior expression that said *I* wouldn't fancy your chances. Then he stepped over to a small table, put down his beer, and took the guitar off his back.

Then sat down to read a newspaper that was lying there already.

After a few more shots of the worst pool imaginable, Ray stepped over to the man and said, 'Are you playing tonight?'

The man looked up from his *Evening Standard* and said, 'Yes, in the basement bar. I'm the headline act.'

'Are you famous?' Ray asked.

'Only in my dreams,' the man said.

'Do you have to pay to get in?'

'No it's free. And the good looking barmaid always works the bar.'

'Hear that Jamie?' Ray said. 'We've got somewhere to go tonight!'

Jamie looked across the pool table and sank a long red. He was thinking he'd like to sink another long red tonight too. Straight into the barmaid with the great tits. He wondered if he could pull it off.

\*\*\*

Jason watched and chatted with the two pool men for about thirty minutes then had to get out of there. The guy called Ray had stood beside his table and told him his whole life story in a ten minute monologue, while his pal Jamie had disappeared to the Gents. Ray was already well oiled and it was only seven-thirty. He told him he worked in IT and was pulling in forty grand a year. Jason wondered if that was really true. Did IT workers really get paid that much? Then he started talking about his work in more detail and Jason's eyes glazed over. There was nothing more boring in the world than computers and Jason certainly didn't want to have a conversation about them. He yawned several times and eventually Jamie returned from the Gents. Then the two of them went back to the pool table and Jason made his escape.

Down in the small basement bar he found Mike setting up the equipment on the low stage and Gill behind the bar tidying up. There were half a dozen others in there too, most of them with guitars.

'I think I've found a couple of suitors for you,' Jason said to Gill, leaning his guitar against the bar. 'They're hot for your body and they're coming down at any moment.'

Gill looked at him and said, 'From the tone of your voice I get the impression I shouldn't get too excited.'

Jason nodded. 'You're spot on. A couple of chancers. I found them in the pool room. You've been warned.'

He bought himself a bottle of Becks and took a sip.

'What time are you on?' Gill asked.

'God knows,' Jason said. 'It's going to be a long night. But I've got a surprise for you. I wrote you a song.'

Gill laughed. 'It's not about my breasts is it?'

Jason smiled. 'Well, they do get a mention. It's called 'Hey Gill'. It was easy to write. Lots of words you can rhyme with Gill.'

'Like, Hey Gill, are you on the pill?'

Jason smiled again. 'That's a good one.'

'Or Hey Gill, are you gonna kill?'

'A bit dark.'

'Hey Gill, I've had my fill. *Now* I'm gonna kill.'

'See it's easy. Anyone can do it.'

'Even a barmaid.'

'Maybe we could co-write someday?'

'That sounds like a euphemism for something else.'

'Maybe.'

Jason could hear voices behind him and then the two guys from upstairs wandered over spoiling the moment. The guy called Ray really was obnoxious, too loud by half and not a trace of subtlety in his conversation. Jason watched protectively over Gill as they ordered their drinks. The guy called Jamie couldn't take his eyes off her. He was wearing one of those T-shirts with the sleeves cut way too short, showing off his impressively tanned arm muscles. Jason found himself staring at the muscles, hard as rock biceps with veins popping out. Maybe if *he* had arms like that Gill would be interested, instead of his middle-aged no-exercise body, with the beginnings of a pot belly. Still, it was too late now. No way was he going to join a gym and start pumping iron. Besides, he had other skills. Like writing songs called 'Hey Gill'. Hey Gill, I've got a lot of skill. No need to kill. Are you really on the pill?

Jason left the bar before Ray could start in on him again and went over to Mike who was on the stage plugging in various leads. Jason knew nothing about the mechanics of setting up a gig and was always impressed by those who could. It always looked so damned complicated: microphones and leads and amps, a never ending tangle of electrical danger. When Jason had first started singing in the late 1970s there had been none of that, just a stool on which to sit, with the audience having to be quiet if they wanted to hear you. Nowadays, with all of the amplification, the audience usually talked loudly while the singer sang. Both situations had their pros and cons and Jason wasn't really sure which he preferred. As long as he got his money he guessed it didn't matter too much either way.

They shook hands and Mike said, 'Ready for another evening of mediocrity?'

Jason nodded. 'I don't know how you do it.'

'I just don't listen. *And* I get paid.'

The evening would start off as an open mic and then Jason would do a set of four songs before the open mic resumed again. Then Jason would finish the evening off with another three songs.

'I hope you listen to *me*,' Jason said, 'I've written a song for Gill called 'Hey Gill'. You'll like it.'

'Yeah? When are you going to write one for me?'

'Like never? Or I could call it, Hey Mike, get on your bike.'

'Sounds good to me,' Mike said, distracted by putting a lead into a black box that looked like something out of a space ship.

Jason wandered off and went behind the sound desk to stash his guitar. The sound man was a bald guy with a ginger beard called Cyril – Jason was amazed that someone would be called Cyril in this day and age – and they exchanged a few pleasantries. Jason never knew what to say to the guy as he was a techno-head and would probably be on some other planet, and didn't they speak their own kind of language anyway? As long as he made Jason sound like a superstar he didn't mind too much. Hey Cyril, you look like a squirrel. He couldn't think of any other rhyme.

At eight o'clock, and with the room only half full, Mike started the evening off by singing a couple of his own songs. Perks of the job. They weren't bad songs, fairly bluesy efforts, just a bit dull lyrically. Mike wasn't a bad picker though, so that made up for it. There was a smattering of applause when he finished and then he introduced the first act, a young guy with a flashy black guitar and long hair who played flashily too and clearly thought he was Peter Frampton. Not that many of the youngsters sitting around would know who Peter Frampton was. Jason sat on a stool at the bar, next to the wall, and listened. He liked watching people sing but it could get tedious after a while if the standard wasn't good. Sometimes he would get a nice surprise though when someone talented got up on stage. But that didn't happen too often. He looked across the bar at Gill serving people. She really was his perfect woman.

*** 

Jamie stood next to his friend Ray and watched as the evening unfolded. He was trying to remember the last time he'd seen live music in a bar. Must be years ago. He found it quite interesting watching all these young people having a go, but why did they do it exactly? Did they think they were going to be famous? Did they think they were on the X Factor? Or were they just showing off to their friends? And why did their new friend Jason do it? He looked way too old to be staying out late at night, getting mixed up in all these shenanigans. He even had grey hair for fucks sake.

Jason came on stage at nine o'clock. Jamie and Ray gave him a few cheers and then fell silent to listen. The bar was now pretty full, nowhere to sit, standing room only. Jason started singing an up tempo song and Jamie was impressed. A nice sound coming from his guitar and a good voice too, not the kind of voice you'd imagine from how he spoke. When the song ended he received a good round of applause and went into the next one. This one was a lot quieter, a slow ballad, something about whisky and cocaine, and Jamie leaned forward to hear.

People were still talking in the bar though and Jamie couldn't understand it. They'd been noisy all evening, except when a girl singer came on stage. Then they'd been respectfully quiet. What the fuck was that all about? Being more polite towards the fairer sex?

'Why are people so noisy?' he said to Ray.

'Because they've got no manners,' Ray said, swigging on probably his tenth bottle of beer.

'Especially this cunt in front of us,' Jamie said.

They were standing behind a fairly tall young man who'd been nattering away all evening with a woman standing next to him. The woman was quite attractive and Jamie had been wondering for the last half hour if he could pull her. He'd been studying her body from behind, a nice figure in a pair of blue jeans. He reached in front of him and tapped the tall guy on the shoulder. The tall guy turned around and Jamie put his forefinger to his lips.

'I'm trying to listen,' he said.

The guy looked at him with a sneer. He had long hair and the wimpy build of a slacker. 'Why don't you go down the front then,' the guy said, then turned and smirked at his girlfriend, raising his eyebrows with disdain.

The temptation was too great. Jamie kicked him hard on his right Achilles with his Dunlop steel toed boots and the guy crumpled to the floor in agony. His girlfriend couldn't believe it.

'What the fuck did you do that for?' she almost screamed at him.

'Cos he's a noisy fucker,' Jamie said. Then, as the girlfriend bent over to help her boyfriend up, Jamie grabbed her arse with his left hand and had a good grope, right down into her crotch area.

The girlfriend couldn't believe it. She turned on him and took a swipe at his face, an attempt that Jamie parried away with ease. Then she tried again, aiming for his eyes with her nails, but Jamie caught both her wrists in a vice-like grip and stood there looking her in the eye. He noticed to his right that Ray was giving the guy on the floor a couple of good kicks too, little digs that no one else would notice.

Jamie started laughing at the woman's attempt at assault. Everyone was turning to look at them and Jason had stopped singing on stage. Lots of people were hurling abuse while Jamie was pressed up against the bar with the woman still trying to gouge his eyes out. She was no problem to fend off though, and he even managed to get a good grope of her tits as well.

After about a minute a black bouncer appeared on the scene and together with the MC guy broke everything up. Jason was sitting on a stool on stage watching the whole thing and shaking his head. The bouncer grabbed Jamie and Ray and shoved them towards the door.

As Jamie passed the stage he shouted up at Jason, 'Great singing my man!'

Jason just looked at him and half a minute later Jamie and Ray were standing out on the street.

'And don't come back. Ever!' the bouncer said to them.

'Don't want to. Ever!' Ray shouted back at him.

The two friends high-fived and walked off down Upper Street laughing their heads off.

## CHAPTER THREE.

On the train ride home Jason went over the evening. More excitement than usual, but also a little depressing. After the ejection of Jamie and Ray he'd done two more songs and then left the stage. At the bar he'd bought another beer and asked Gill what the hell had gone on.

'Your two new friends started a ruckus,' she said. 'The one with the muscles kicked the guy in front of him for talking through your act. Then the guy's girlfriend chipped in.'

'Jesus,' Jason said. 'I knew that guy was no good the moment I laid eyes on him. Never trust a guy who's got his muscles on show.'

'That's my motto,' Gill said. 'Give me a skinny guy any day.'

'With grey hair?'

Gill looked at his hair and said, 'Yes, it doesn't bother me.'

The rest of the evening had passed without incident. Jason had finished the evening by singing 'Hey Gill' plus two up tempo songs including 'I Fought the Law (and the law won)' which he'd dedicated with irony to the two troublemakers from earlier. That had got a few laughs. Then he'd picked up his £20 from Mike and said goodbye to Gill. She'd told him that she liked her song and could he sing it again for her next time? Jason said he would and left her behind the bar to clear up. He always felt a bit sorry for her working so late. It wasn't a safe way for a woman to make a living. Especially one who was so good looking.

Sitting in a packed tube with late night revellers, Jason smiled at Gill's grey hair comment, wondering if he really might be in with a chance. He had asked her out once before, must be about a year ago now, and she'd turned him down. Maybe he should try again, ask her in a casual way so it wouldn't look too bad if she said no again. He had her mobile number; he could do it by text, the coward's way. He wasn't sure when he was next at the pub, probably in a couple of weeks.

His hair had started going grey about a decade ago, right after the incidents in Woodvale and then Cambridge involving the violent criminal Teddy Peppers. Peppers had been released from jail after a stint for armed robbery, then travelled to Woodvale looking for Jason, intent on getting some revenge for the death of his prison buddy Phil Gator. Gator had been killed in Jason's house by the ex-criminal and wanted man Frankie Bosser; beaten up in Jason's first floor bedroom, then thrown off the balcony on to the concrete terrace below. Gator had been on the rampage in Woodvale and Redgate killing how many people in total? About five Jason seemed to remember. Gator had also broken Jason's right thumb when he was torturing him, before Frankie Bosser arrived on the scene to save him. His thumb had never really been the same since, though it hadn't affected his guitar playing too much. Then Peppers had arrived on the scene and all the violence had flared up again, more dead bodies and a showdown on the River Cam in Cambridge on a couple of punts. Jason still couldn't believe it had all happened. Sometimes life was just too crazy for words. And the shock of it all had turned his hair grey. Now it was almost silver, which didn't look too bad really.

He tried to kid himself that he looked like that cool dude with the silver hair in *Mad Men*, the one that was always cheating on his wife. Or maybe Ted Danson when he was in *Damages*. Yes grey hair could look good on some people. A couple of years ago Jason had gone to a school reunion somewhere down in Surrey, and one of his old girlfriends had turned up with grey hair. She had looked stunning. Yes grey hair could definitely be cool.

He looked at himself in the reflection of the tube window when a few people got off. He could remember when he was in his late teens studying the same reflection when he used to travel into London from the suburbs for his first forays into the big city, spending the day in the West End looking in music shops and going home with books of sheet music and LPs. Those had been good days full of hope and excitement, learning new songs on his guitar and wishing that one day he would make a living as a folk singer, like Bob Dylan or Gordon Lightfoot or Jim Croce. Now here he was at the age of fifty-two, facially not that much different, but with the silver hair that he kept fairly long, over his ears and down to his shoulders, trying to make up for the greyness with extra length. He was beginning to look like those old rockers on BBC4 music documentaries reliving the good old days of rock and roll and hedonism, except he didn't look as rough as them. He had never really indulged in drugs that much and he wasn't much of a drinker anymore, had never been too indulgent with that either. Nowadays he was quite happy with a few beers or a few glasses of wine, or better still, nothing. You had to be careful the older you got – or there sure as hell would be no chance of getting off with women like Gill.

After forty-five minutes on the tube Jason finally arrived at Turnham Green station. He headed right and crossed the road by the Tabard theatre pub, then took the second left down Highsmith Road. He was home within five minutes, unlocking the door to a large Victorian house, then stepping over to the ground floor door of flat number one. He liked living at number one; it gave him hope that one day he would have a number one song. Or be the number one man to a woman like Gill.

Leaning his guitar case against the wall, Jason drew the living room curtains on the bay windows and turned on the lights. Then he walked into the kitchen, turned the kettle on for a cup of tea, and made himself a sandwich of tuna mayonnaise even though it was well after midnight. He hadn't eaten anything since six o'clock, except for a packet of crisps, bought for him by Ray before his ejection. Jason often thought of taking a sandwich with him to gigs but it seemed like such an un-cool thing to do, like he was some kind of pensioner on a day trip. He had to look as hip as possible, even if he was fifty-two with grey hair.

The kitchen was a decent size and full of too much stuff that he'd accumulated over the last two years. He liked to buy crockery in charity shops, couldn't resist another mug or wine glass or whisky goblet, and his collection of condiments was something to be proud of. Being a single man for most of his life his cooking was pretty good, and he had quite a long list of menus stored away in his head that he could rustle up for himself or whichever woman he was going out with. Not that he'd been out with a woman for a while. In fact he hadn't been laid for about a year, something that didn't bother him as much as he thought it would. After all, he was approaching old age. It was inevitable that sex was going to taper off into the forgotten past.

With his sandwich and tea Jason sat at the dining table in the living room and turned on his computer. He logged on to the Internet and checked his emails. The first guitar lesson of tomorrow had been cancelled by one of his less diligent pupils, which was a relief. That meant he wouldn't have to get up so early. After that he went on to Wikipedia and put Sara Shriver into search. She came up straightaway and he started to read.

She was born only two years later than him so was now fifty. Amazing. He looked down at her list of film credits and counted off about five that he'd seen, mainly B movie type crime films which he usually enjoyed. When he looked at her personal life he was amazed to see 'she currently lives in West London with her film producer husband David Paxton'. So she really did live in Chiswick. Jason was thrilled.

There was an even bigger shock right at the bottom of the article. 'Sara Shriver currently plays in her own country band called The Shrivers. They have recorded one CD called *From W4 With Twang*, and played last year at the Celtic Connections Festival in Glasgow, and at SXSW in Austin, Texas'. Wow, Jason thought. She's a musician too! The coincidences were piling up. And the title of her CD was a giveaway. W4 was a Chiswick postcode. So she really did live there. Maybe if he bumped into her again he could give her one of his CDs, ask if she wanted to record one of his songs. Or maybe they could have a jam together. It could be the start of a beautiful friendship. He'd never hung out with a film star before.

He logged on to Spotify, put in the name of her band, and found her CD. On the cover she was wearing a very low cut top, quite a lot of cleavage on show. Jason was a bit surprised about that. Most serious women artists these days wouldn't have such a flirty cover. Especially if they were fifty. He clicked on one of the songs and had a listen. It was a slow country ballad with her voice quite low in the mix so he could hardly make out the words. He listened to a couple of more songs and nothing really stood out. The songs were pretty forgettable in fact, all about babies and motherhood as far as he could make out. Hardly cutting edge material. Maybe she could do with another songwriter on board. He would definitely have to speak to her next time he saw her. But when would that be? It might not be for another year, or maybe never.

Jason yawned. It was time to go to bed. He closed the computer down, went to the bathroom to clean his teeth – too tired to floss – and then took out his contact lenses.

In the bedroom he undressed quickly and got under the duvet wearing just his boxers. He turned off the bedside light and closed his eyes thinking about two women, Gill and Sara. It had been an interesting day. He was asleep within five minutes.

## CHAPTER FOUR.

'If my life was an American movie,' Glenn said, 'this scene that I'm going to tell you about would be laden with heavy meaning, filmed in slow motion with a bit of soft focus. But we British don't think about things very deeply, so it isn't. We dismiss them out of hand, or keep them to ourselves, and then head for the pub.'

Scobie looked at him blankly. He didn't have a clue what he was on about.

Glenn continued. 'So this is what happened. It was 1963. I was seven years old and I was walking through the streets of Redgate with my old man. It was a busy Saturday afternoon and we were just off the high street heading to I don't know where. As the streets were crowded I reached out to grab my dad's hand and walked a few steps before looking up to see that the hand didn't belong to my dad but to another man instead, a complete stranger. The man looked down at me and smiled and let go of my hand. My dad came over and the two of them laughed about it while I stood there feeling very foolish and embarrassed. They chatted for about half a minute and then we went our separate ways.'

Glenn sipped his pint. Scobie was listening to his story at least. Glenn had told it to so many people over the years, and amazingly it was true. 'Later that same year one of the biggest crimes in British history was committed, The Great Train Robbery in which a gang of robbers stole 2.6 million pounds from a mail train. Worth about 46 million in today's money. The whole nation was gripped by the drama and my dad watched the news every night to see when the criminals would be caught. About five weeks later the criminals were finally apprehended and their photos were splashed across our TV screens and newspapers. On seeing the photos for the first time at the breakfast table, my dad looked over at me and said, "Well I never." He passed the paper to me and said, "Do you remember this man Glenn?" I looked down at the photo and said no.'

Glenn paused for effect. 'My dad said, "This was the man whose hand you grabbed in the street a few months ago. Remember?" I looked back down at the photo and still didn't remember. Why would I? The whole episode had only lasted a few seconds and had already been consigned to the past, and being only seven, I rarely went back over my past. After all, there wasn't that much of it.'

'Plenty of time later to look back at the past,' Scobie said.

Glenn nodded half-heartedly. He didn't want Scobie to interrupt his flow. 'My mother came over to the table then and looked down at the photo. "Ronald Biggs," she said. "A carpenter from Redgate. Interesting."'

'My dad smiled at me. "Looks like you've been touched by crime young Glenn," he said. "I hope that isn't an omen." I shrugged and went back to my breakfast of toast and marmalade. I didn't really know what they were on about. But now, many years later, this episode would be laden with significance, especially if it was in an American movie. One of those prologues to catch the viewer's attention. The picture would go hazy then...Fade into the present day. Glenn Swell, career criminal on the run. Touched by crime all those years ago.'

Scobie creased his forehead, puzzled. 'Except you're not on the run, are you?'

'No I'm not,' Glenn said. 'I'm sitting here with you. But if it was a movie, you'd be a good looking woman and I'd be on the run from something. Got to make it more interesting. Grab the viewer's attention.'

Scobie nodded. 'The great Ronnie Biggs. That's impressive. I knew he was living around here at the time. I wonder where exactly. I'd like to find that out.'

'Just look it up on the Internet. It's probably on there somewhere.'

'Fuck the Internet. I've got better things to do with my time. So what happened next?'

'What do you mean what happened next?'

'After you were touched by crime. The hand of rob. Geddit? The hand of rob. Short for robber.'

Glenn shook his head. 'Very witty. After being touched by Mr Biggs I carried on with my schooling and left at the age of sixteen. I went to work in the local factories of Redgate.'

'Yeah? But I thought you drifted into a life of crime.'

'Yes I did. But that came a little later. You really want to know?'

'Of course I do. It's not everyday you come across a real life criminal. I want to know.'

Glenn took a sip of his pint. It was early evening and they were sitting in the Home Cottage pub at the bottom of Redgate Hill. Glenn had been going there for years, first as a sixteen year old and now as a fifty-eight year old. The only years he'd skipped were those he'd been inside, about seventeen years in total for various kinds of armed robbery.

'It all started when I was seventeen,' he said. 'I was working in a tool factory on the Holmethorpe Industrial Estate as an apprentice and I started nicking tools. I got away with it for a few months, then got caught and got the sack. Also got my first criminal conviction.'

'Stealing tools and what?' Scobie asked. 'Selling them on?' Scobie was an overweight taxi driver, spent every day sitting on his arse in his car down at Redgate station waiting for fares. He worked about fourteen hours a day – that's if you could call it work, sitting in your car reading a newspaper most of the time – and just about broke even. He had a wife and two kids to support too.

'Yeah. I used to take them around to garages in my spare time, riding a little moped, a bag of tools strapped on the back. What a loser. I hardly made any money at all and the fine I got just about wiped away all of the profit.'

'So what happened next?'

'I got another job, this time in a plastics factory on the estate, and I laid low for a couple of years. But then I got bored again and went into armed robbery.'

'Wow,' Scobie said. 'Like it was almost meant to be. Touched by Biggs, turned to armed robbery. You couldn't make it up.'

You *could* make it up Glenn thought. Like they did in all those American films. They had imagination. Unlike British films.

'I joined a little gang that specialised in robbing jewellery stores. I was twenty at the time. There were four of us, two of us on motorbikes. We'd ride up to the stores in broad daylight and the other two would jump off the back and go inside with their hammers and bags. Me and my pal Dougie would block the doorway with our bikes and wait for the other two to come back out. Would only take a couple of minutes. Then we'd ride off into the sunset. We did four within a month and then got caught. I was sent away for four years.'

'Jesus. You must have had some balls to do that.' There was a look of awe on Scobie's face. They had only known each other about a month, Glenn coming down to the Home Cottage for a beer and ending up in a game of darts with people he'd never met before. Though he'd lived in Redgate all his life, his childhood friends had moved away, getting married and moving to better areas of Surrey or Sussex or Kent. And because of his criminal past a lot of people knew about him and avoided him.

They were scared of him. Scobie for instance, would be fine for a couple of months and then something would happen or he'd hear some story that wasn't necessarily true, and Glenn would never see him again. That's just the way things happened. Glenn made people uncomfortable. He didn't really give a shit though. Their loss, he always thought.

Of course, he could just keep quiet about his criminal past to every new person that he met, but it would come out eventually. Someone would take Scobie or whoever aside and say 'Do you know who that is?' or 'Do you know what he did?' And bla bla bla it would all be revealed, exaggerated of course, tall stories made even taller by the passing of the years. He was a living legend in Redgate, one that most people would rather see as a dead legend. He could feel it every time he walked into a bar. The sudden hush, the turning of heads, the whispered remarks. So be it. Maybe he should have moved away from the area years ago but home was home. You had to put roots down somewhere.

'You get used to it,' Glenn said. 'Balls doesn't really come into it. You're just a kid trying to have some fun. It's exciting. And even more exciting when you get the payoff. Then you can live like a king for a few weeks. Lots of booze and lots of women.'

'But then you get caught and you have to live like a nobody for four years.'

Glenn shrugged. 'That's the downside. You make some new friends, learn a few new tricks. You come out a much more knowledgeable criminal than when you went in. That's the plus side. Then you go back to work.'

'So what was next on the agenda?'

'More of the same. Stick to what you know. Of course, once you come out of jail it's nigh on impossible to find a job so you just drift into crime again. I was free for a couple of years and then went back inside. For six years.'

'Jesus,' Scobie said again. 'Jewellery stores again?'

Glenn shook his head. 'I did a few more of those but didn't get caught. The next time was for a security van.'

The crime in question was a quick smash and grab of a security van while they were loading up their money outside of a Tesco's. Wielding a machete in his right hand, Glenn had marched up to a scared looking security guard who had almost shit his pants before dropping the hard case with all the money in it. Glenn had run down the road to his escape car, driven by his buddy Malcolm, only to be cut off by three police cars in the next village along. If Malcolm had been a better driver they would probably have gotten away with it, but Malcolm had driven too cautiously, even stopping for red lights along the way. He'd only received two years in jail while Glenn had rotted away for six. Sometimes crime just wasn't fair.

'Anyway, I won't bore you with the details,' Glenn said. 'Once you're on that merry-go-round it's pretty hard to get off. I've had occasional jobs along the way, mostly on building sites. Now at last I am off. I live a normal life on benefits. I have one grown up kid. I want to be respectable for him.'

'And where does he live?' Scobie asked.

'In London. No crime in his life. Not that I know of anyway.' Glenn sniggered. 'Let's play some darts.'

The dartboard was free so the two of them went up for a game. The only problem playing with Scobie was that his maths was no good. He couldn't subtract the scores on the blackboard so Glenn had to do all of the scoring himself. Which was kind of annoying. Plus the fat fuck was such a slow walker, back and forth to the board, things took forever. And if one of his darts ended up on the floor, forget about it, it took a major effort for him to bend down and pick it up, so Glenn saved time by picking it up for him. Just like a servant. He wondered how people got into such a state of unfitness. Did they have such a low opinion of themselves that they just had to eat and eat all the time and not take any exercise? Surely there was a point somewhere in between where you would think, hey, I'm getting a little fat here, I'd better slam on the breaks. Not go hell for leather right to the end of the fat line. Fat people disgusted Glenn if he had to be honest. How did Scobie even manage to fit on the toilet when he took a dump? His ass was so big he'd need a crapper twice the size.

As far as Glenn's own body was concerned, he was still pretty fit for a fifty-eight year old. He did press ups and sit ups everyday, so his body was still hard as rock. He had a slight beer belly but nothing to worry about. In a baggy jumper you couldn't notice it at all. And he still had a good head of hair though it was quickly turning grey.

He was shrinking in height though. He was sure he used to be close to six feet, but nowadays he reckoned he was about five ten. That just wasn't fair. Not only did you get old, you also shrivelled away. He was convinced his dick was getting smaller too. He had measured it a few weeks ago with a ruler and erect it was now only six inches long. He was sure it had been seven inches when he was in his twenties.

He thrashed Scobie 3-0 at darts then said he was going home. He was bored with playing in slow motion. Scobie looked a little hurt as he slumped down in a chair, out of breath just from walking backwards and forwards to the board. Glenn took a final piss and left the pub.

He was currently living in a tiny bed-sit down the other end of Frenches Road, a good fifteen minute walk away. He stepped out into the warm summer evening and took a few swigs of whisky from a metal hip flask hidden in his jacket pocket. He went everywhere with his flask these days. It belonged to an old girlfriend of his and had a big dent right down the middle, but the dent actually made it fit into his pocket better. As he no longer had to work, permanently scrounging off the government these days, he didn't mind being juiced up most of the time. And what was the worst that could happen? A heart attack. End his life ten years prematurely. He wouldn't be missing much. He could handle it.

He walked down the hill and under the railway bridge by the station, then turned right for Frenches. It was ironic that he was now living on the road right next to the Holmethorpe Industrial Estate where he'd first started his working life. He was literally right across the road from the entrance, the short tunnel that went under the railway tracks.

As he approached his building he hoped that his two neighbours were tucked up safely in bed or watching TV. They were an odd couple called Vernon and Daisy. They were both in their mid to late thirties and had more rows than Glenn could reasonably deal with. Daisy was permanently ill – Glenn had never found out with what exactly – so took medication that turned her either aggressive or passive. The pills also made her face swell in mysterious ways, so sometimes she looked completely different to other times, like a grotesquely shaped potato or turnip, sometimes bright red, sometimes brown, very rarely normal.

Vernon was a short muscle-bound man who worked in either a garage or factory, Glenn had never cared for the details. You could tell he was the pussy in the relationship because it was always Daisy who sounded in control in the arguments, Vernon ranting and raving and saying things like

'You never loved me!' and 'I'm going to kill myself!' From his tiny room upstairs listening to these outpourings, Glenn had often answered back 'Just go ahead and do it then loser, then I'll kill Daisy and have the whole house to myself.' It was a situation he often fantasised about and probably the only way he was going to get a house to himself at this late stage of his life. They all rented out to the same landlord, an elderly gentleman who lived about fifty yards down the road. Maybe Glenn could kill him too, end up with an extra house for his son. It was something to think about.

He opened the street door and stepped quietly into the front hall. There was another resident on the ground floor, some old duffer who Glenn rarely saw, whose entrance was at the back of the house in the garden.

Glenn dreaded walking up the first flight of stairs, then walking past the three doors of Vernon and Daisy's abode in case one of them came out to greet him. First the kitchen, then their bedroom, then their living room. All was silent thankfully, so he went up to the top floor.

Glenn's room was next door to the bathroom which he shared with Vernon and Daisy. He went inside for a final piss and then unlocked the door to his room which was even smaller than his various prison cells had been. All he had in there was a single bed, a metal table, one wardrobe, a cabinet for kitchen goods, and in the corner by the window a sink and a Baby Belling cooker. At the end of the bed he had one armchair which faced a 12" TV that sat on a chair. What made the room feel even smaller was its sloping ceiling which in winter dripped with condensation. Two winters ago Glenn had started coughing badly, a racking cough that had quickly turned into pleurisy. He'd spent an agonising few weeks in bed popping penicillin pills until the pain had gone. It was one of the few times in his life when he wished he was dead. He knew he would have to get out of the room sooner rather than later. Two winters in there was enough.

He stripped down to his underpants and climbed into the lumpy bed. He felt like an early night. By the light of his bedside lamp he read ten pages of a Robert Ludlum novel then turned it off and went to sleep.

He dreamed of a better future in a land faraway. Somewhere like Australia would be far enough, but what were the chances of that happening? Less than zero would be about right.

## *CHAPTER FIVE.*

It was only about a month later when he saw her once again. It was as if their lives were meant to be entwined - his own and a film star, who just happened to live in his particular area of London.

Jason was riding on the District Line one afternoon, having just completed two guitar lessons in the Earl's Court area. Some pupils preferred it if he visited their homes (especially if they were young), so they paid extra for his travel and off he went. He didn't mind too much. It got him out of his flat and seeing different parts of London. And now, on this particular afternoon, he was thanking his lucky stars, because here once again was Sara Shriver.

He hadn't noticed her when he'd first got on the train, had merely made a beeline for a vacant seat. Then, when the train pulled into Turnham Green station, he'd stood up with his guitar, turned to his right, and there she was, standing up at the same time as him, her guitar slung over her shoulder and a small suitcase on wheels by her feet. She was only about ten feet away, wearing jeans, sweater and trainers. They turned towards each other and both of them smiled at the same time. It was clearly meant to be.

Jason walked towards her and said, 'How's the music going?' Afterwards he couldn't believe how brave he'd been. Normally he would shy away from such a situation, let the moment pass and regret it forever. Yet there he was, talking to Ms Shriver as if she was a long lost friend. And maybe she was.

'It's going good,' Sara replied with her soft American accent. 'How about you?'

The tube doors opened and they both stepped out on to the station. Then they stood there looking at each other.

'Also going good,' Jason said. 'I teach guitar. Just taken a couple of lessons near Earl's Court.'

'Teach guitar? That's impressive. Maybe you could give me a few lessons.'

'Maybe I could,' Jason said. 'Always touting for more business.'

He could sense people looking at them as they made their way to the stairs that led down to the station's exit. It felt good walking along beside someone famous.

'Need help with your suitcase?' Jason asked.

'No it's okay,' Sara said. 'I'm getting used to the life of the travelling musician these days.'

Jason wondered how much he should let on that he knew about her. He decided to go full steam ahead once they were at the bottom of the stairs. 'I read about you on the Internet,' he said. 'I saw you walking past the station one day and was amazed to see you. I didn't know that you lived in London.'

Now they were at the ticket barrier. They passed through and walked to the entrance. 'I moved here about ten years ago,' Sara Shriver said. 'I like London. Plus I have my long running TV series over here.'

'Yes, I knew you were in that,' Jason said. 'Though I must be the only person who hasn't watched it.' They stopped outside the station. 'Which way are you going?'

Sara pointed. 'To the right.'

'Same as me,' Jason said. 'I'd really like to have a chat with you about some songs.'

Sara Shriver laughed. 'Are you going to pitch me your latest song? I've read about that happening if you're Johnny Cash or someone. Do you happen to have a CD with you?'

'No,' Jason said. 'But I can get one to you pretty quick.'

As they walked he told her about his two CDs and also about his various tours, just so she'd know that he wasn't a stalker or psycho. She seemed to be impressed and knew all the singers he'd performed with. And why shouldn't she? They were all well known within the country field.

'If I Google your name will it come up?' she asked.

'You'll find my CD on there,' Jason said. 'I have my own website. But my name is quite common so I'm pretty hard to find. Also, my tours were back in the dark ages, before the Internet really got going. I didn't even have the Internet until about 2001. How about you?'

'Probably the same. Life was so much simpler then. None of this Twitter and Facebook. Are you on Twitter?'

'No. Are you?'

'Yes, I'm afraid so. I only use it for promotion though. Nothing personal.'

'Sensible.'

'Yes. Too many people get caught out by it. Who needs a nasty surprise?'

Not me, Jason thought. Too many of those in the old days.

He was amazed to discover that Sara was heading home in the same direction that he would normally go. Up Highsmith Road and then onto Fareham. Did they in fact live quite near each other?

'Where do you live exactly?' he asked. 'This is the same route I take home.'

'At the end of Fareham,' Sara said.

'Amazing. I live just around the corner on Willeford.'

'So we're neighbours. That'll come in handy for when you want to pitch me some songs.' Sara smiled at him.

Jason couldn't believe how well this was going. Sara was such a nice lady. Must be her southern manners. Hadn't she been born in New Orleans? He seemed to remember from Wikipedia.

Five minutes later they were standing outside a large house on the corner of Fareham. The building looked quite similar to Jason's, though he was willing to bet it wasn't divided into flats and that Sara and her husband owned the whole thing.

'That's my door,' Sara said. 'Just drop a CD through the letterbox anytime. It was nice meeting you.'

'Likewise,' Jason said. They shook hands. 'I'll put all my details on the CD. Maybe we could meet up sometime for a jam.'

'Or a guitar lesson.'

'Right. I charge double for film stars.'

Sara laughed and then turned for her door. Jason watched her for a second then carried on home.

\*\*\*

He spent the rest of the day on a high. He couldn't believe what had just happened. He couldn't wait to see Sara Shriver again, swap some songs, sing a few duets. Maybe she would invite him on tour. He could be her Rodney Crowell. She could be his Emmylou. With his stronger songs maybe her star would rise. Or maybe he was getting ahead of himself.

He still had three more lessons to get through that evening. The first was a Polish woman in her thirties who picked things up quickly but never practised enough. His second was a manual worker whose fingers were so thick he struggled to find the right chords. And his third was a long haired slacker guy who wrote John Martyn type songs but was always more interested in performing them than learning about guitar. By nine o'clock the day was over. Jason fixed himself a snack and went back on the Internet to have another look at Sara Shriver.

He Googled her 'images' and had a look at all the photos. If you were a famous film star your photo got taken so many times it was unreal. Photos from film premieres, walking along the red carpet, or at film festivals, and of course hundreds of stills from films. Sara had been a beautiful woman when she was younger, still was in her fifties, though Jason had noticed up close the signs of middle-age making their mark; her eyelids sagging a bit, also her jowls. He knew these things well; it had been happening to him just lately too.

For the hell of it Jason put into Google images 'Sara Shriver topless'. He was amazed by how many photos came up. Obviously she hadn't minded taking her top off when she was younger, or maybe it was just the same few film stills repeated over and over. Jason came to the conclusion that it was probably only about four films in total.

He checked his emails and Facebook. He didn't know why he bothered with the latter these days. Nobody said anything of interest anymore. Maybe he should go on Twitter. It seemed to be the latest fad. A good way of putting your news across to thousands of followers. But how did you get thousands of followers? Jason couldn't see the point of ordinary people being on it at all. It was just a quicker form of Facebook.

As an afterthought he Googled Sara Shriver's Twitter account and up it came. That was another thing he didn't like about Twitter – anyone could read what you said, even non-members. He was amazed to see that her latest entry read, 'Someone just tried to pitch me some songs in the street. That's a first!'

Jason chuckled. Sara was still thinking about him. With that satisfied thought, he logged off and went to bed.

# CHAPTER SIX.

On the streets of Islington, north London, Jamie and Ray were once again on a night out. They met up about once a month, and it had been a month or so since their ejection from The Hope and Anchor for causing a fight during the open mic. With a few beers already in their bellies they were in the mood for adventure once again.

Ray said, 'Why don't we try the open mic again. Turn it into an open fight. See if they remember us.'

'They *will* remember us,' Jamie said. 'Bound to. Especially if the same bouncer is on the door.'

'It might be his night off,' Ray said. 'Maybe Jason will be there. I'm sure he'd like to see us again.'

'Yeah right. Did you see his face when they threw us out? Like he didn't want to know us. Like we were a couple of turds.'

'I didn't notice. I was too revved up.'

'I would quite like to see him again though,' Jamie said. 'I've been thinking about taking guitar lessons.'

Ray laughed loudly. '*That* I would like to see. You and your muscles playing guitar. What kind of songs would you sing? You don't even like music!'

'I like music. We've just never talked about it.'

'Like what?'

Jamie had to think about that one. 'Pop songs. Chart stuff. I reckon if I could play the guitar I could pull women easier. Isn't that what they all say?'

'Ah, so now we're getting to it. You want to use a guitar as a pulling machine.'

'Kind of. I wouldn't get up on no stage though. Fuck that.'

'No, I couldn't imagine you on stage.' Ray let out a loud laugh again.

They had just had a burger meal in the O2 centre, probably the worst burger that Jamie had ever eaten. It had included bacon and a fried egg slapped on top of the burger, with chips and salad on the side. The burger had been burnt as well, giving it an overall shite taste. At over £8 Jamie had been tempted to send it back. Burgers were turning into pizzas; just throw anything in the kitchen on top of them, when the best way was just to keep it simple. Jamie sometimes wondered if he should be on TV. He could teach the world a few things about cooking. Just like his namesake Jamie Oliver.

They were now walking down Upper Street, the road that never ended. They passed restaurants and pubs with locals and tourists sitting at pavement tables to eat, something that Jamie could never imagine doing. He could never understand the attraction of eating on pavements when cars were driving by just a few feet away blowing their fumes all over you. Not to mention homeless people hassling you for money as well. He was also too much of an outsider and always felt uncomfortable in restaurants. The whole idea of someone serving him food just didn't sit right with him. In the burger bar they'd just been to it was a case of going to the counter and ordering the food themselves, then a waiter brought it over. That was a better way of doing things. It also meant you didn't look mean if you didn't tip. Jamie felt uncomfortable tipping too. Ten percent or fifteen? It was just a whole lot easier not to go into restaurants at all, go to McDonald's instead, you didn't have to tip staff in there. But Ray liked going to restaurants so Jamie tagged along. Ray earned good money so felt he deserved the occasional meal out. Jamie didn't care one way or the other what Ray spent his money on. If he wanted to waste £20 or more on a meal, that was his choice.

They had met the previous year when Jamie was doing a computer course, a free one provided by the Job Centre. Though Ray had a decent 'proper' job in IT, somewhere in The City, he occasionally did a bit of computer teaching as well, spreading his knowledge to the less fortunate. Jamie had never heard of an IT person caring about other people, had always thought of them as selfish money grabbers, but Ray put himself across as something else, a bit of a do-gooder on the side. Jamie didn't believe it for a second. After all, why would a do-gooder get involved in bar fights? It just didn't make sense, and they'd had several skirmishes since they'd known each other.

The first had been in another Islington bar during a football match involving Arsenal. Islington was an Arsenal area, and one evening when the local team had been playing an important European match televised in all the bars, Jamie and Ray had become too vocal, supporting the opposing side, Barcelona if he remembered correctly, and the Spanish side had won the game by about four goals to one. Towards the end of the game Ray had been laughing and hurling abuse at the TV screen and had received a tap on his shoulder from a big displeased Arsenal fan. Ray had told him to fuck off and a bit of pushing and shoving had ensued. A bouncer had intervened before things kicked off and Jamie and Ray had been escorted outside. Jamie had been relieved. If a fight had started up they would have been seriously outnumbered and a good beating would have been the only outcome.

That had been his first experience of the darker side of Ray Lane and several weeks later he saw it again. This time the encounter took place in a West End pub called The Spice of Life, down in the basement bar. As closing time neared one of the barmen kept pestering them to leave and Ray just snapped and attacked the guy. They'd ended up on the floor punching the shit out of each other, about ten customers just sitting there watching. The pub didn't have any bouncers so the fight just continued until eventually Jamie thought he'd better stop it. He'd pulled Ray off the man, told him to calm down, and that was another pub they'd been banned from.

Jamie often wondered what it would be like to have a fight with Ray. He was one of those crazy people who just lost it, 'it' being all fear and reason, like a bull in a china shop. Ray was overweight and totally unfit, but once he got swinging he could cause some damage. Jamie on the other hand, was supremely fit. He went to the gym about four times a week, lifted weights, cycled and ran on machines, in fact did any machine that looked worth doing. And though he now had great muscles, he had never really been a fighter and had always avoided it in the past. But now, hanging out with Ray, he could see the appeal of it, how it could spice up an evening (The Spice of Life!) instead of the usual just wandering home half-cut, with nothing to show for it except an empty wallet.

The Hope and Anchor incident had really been Jamie's first foray into the unknown, that quick kick into that guy's Achilles. And where had he learnt that little move from? He had no idea. Maybe he'd seen it in a film or something, though he knew the Achilles was a painful sports injury to get, so maybe it was also a painful one to inflict. And the guy had just collapsed as if he'd been shot. Amazing. He would like to try it again sometime on another unsuspecting loser.

They came to The Hope and Anchor and stood outside looking through the window.

'There's that barmaid again,' Ray said. 'The one with the tits.'

Jamie nodded, looking through the glass at the luscious sight. She was bound to remember them. He really wanted to go inside and say hello, maybe apologise and see if she accepted. Then maybe ask her out. He really wished he had a guitar to sling over his shoulder. That would impress her. She'd think he was a sensitive soul then, even if he couldn't play it.

'I've got an idea,' he said to Ray. 'Let's go to The Library. I think there's an open mic on there tonight.'

'Okay,' Ray said. 'Whatever you want.'

They wandered farther up the road and a few minutes later The Library came into view. They had never been there before, had never fancied a pub with such a boring name. And when they walked through the door they saw just why it was called that. On one wall there were shelves holding red leather-bound hardback copies of books. And some of the customers were even reading.

'Fuck me,' Ray said. 'We're really getting in touch with our sensitive side aren't we? First you tell me you want to play guitar, and now this. Books!'

'Amazing,' Jamie said. 'Who'd have thunk it.'

'Who indeed.' Ray then looked at the pictures on the walls. 'But also photos of semi-nude dancers. Interesting.'

'I think they call them exotic these days.'

'Or maybe just plain fucking weird,' Ray said.

They went to the bar and ordered a pint each, asked the hairy barman where the open mic was.

'Upstairs,' he said, looking them over, not too friendly.

Ray said, 'Do we have to pay?' and the barman looked at him like he was an idiot and laughed.

They found the stairs and up they went. They could hear the music straightaway and Jamie said, 'I recognise that voice don't you?'

Ray shook his head.

'Jason,' Jamie said. 'If I'm not mistaken.'

'Rock on,' Ray said.

'Too right,' Jamie said. 'Now I can get my guitar lessons booked.'

## *CHAPTER SEVEN.*

Jason was on the penultimate song of his first half of the show when he noticed the two walking in. He almost forgot the words, but being a pro managed to get through the song and finish. Then as a joke, he decided to once again sing 'I Fought the Law', just as he'd done the night Jamie and Ray had been ejected from The Hope and Anchor. He even dedicated it to them, both of them turning towards him from the bar area and giving him the thumbs up.

Later, Jason wondered why he had mentioned them at all. He knew they were bad news and not the kind of guys he should be mixing with, especially at his age. But it had been a quiet evening so far, only about twenty people in the venue coming and going. Maybe the two of them would liven things up.

When he left the stage he went over to them both and a bottle of Becks was stuck in his hand by Ray. Jamie asked him what that song was that he'd just sung. Jason told him and Jamie said, 'I want to learn it. Can you teach me?'

'Of course,' Jason said. 'It's easy. Just three chords.'

'What's a chord?' Jamie asked.

'The way you hold your left hand,' Jason said. 'I could teach you that song in thirty minutes. It would take you longer than that to practice though.'

Ray chipped in with, 'Jamie thinks it'll help him to pick up women. When he learns a musical instrument.'

Jason nodded. He'd heard that rumour many times before. Had it ever helped him pick up a woman though? Well yes, it probably had.

He reached in his jeans pocket and brought out his wallet. Took out a business card and handed it to Jamie. 'Just give me a ring sometime or send me an email. We can set up a date. Where do you live?'

'Camden,' Jamie said. 'Will I have to buy me a guitar?'

'It would help. Or we could buy one together sometime if you like. I know a few shops. Don't want you buying an expensive one in case you don't enjoy it.'

'Great,' Jamie said. 'I can feel this'll be my new thing. My new hobby.'

'Everyone needs a hobby,' Ray said, a big smirk on his face. 'I like baking cakes myself.'

Jason and Jamie looked at him. Jason couldn't tell if he was being serious or not. Probably was. Ever since *The Great British Bake Off* had started on TV he suspected the whole country was baking cakes.

Jamie looked at his friend and said, 'That's probably why you're such a fat fuck then.'

Ray looked a little hurt and said, 'Yeah probably.'

Jason knew it was time to move on. He said, 'I'll see you both later,' and moved over to some of his more regular friends.

\*\*\*

Jamie and Ray continued drinking. They watched the other singers performing, most of them singing heartfelt songs they'd written themselves that went on for far too long.

'These songs need some serious editing,' Ray said. 'Like maybe four minutes worth.'

'Too right,' Jamie said. 'Whatever happened to the three minute single?'

'I blame it all on Nick Drake,' Ray said.

'Who's Nick Drake?'

'An English guy who wrote long songs about his inner torment and then died young.'

Jamie nodded. 'I can see the attraction of dying young. Having a good looking corpse.'

'Yeah,' Ray said. 'You'd look good in your coffin, but you wouldn't be able to appreciate it. I'd rather be old and ugly. Get my money's worth.'

'Well, you've got half of that already,' Jamie joked.

Ray smiled, a little hurt again. 'Take Amy Winehouse for instance. Do you think she's in heaven looking down and saying, "At least I had a good looking corpse."'

'Point taken. I wouldn't call her good looking though. She was far too skinny.'

'She was good looking when she was younger. Before she got into all those drugs.'

'True. I've seen pictures.'

Ray took a long sip of his drink. 'It's like these footballers looking up to the heavens when they score as if someone up there can see them. Or Andy

Murray when he looks to the sky when he's won a match. So fucking phoney. I feel like saying to them "No one can see you tosser. They're dead. Celebrate with the living."'

Jamie nodded.

'So fuck the good looking corpse routine,' Ray carried on. 'Enjoy it down here. While you have it.'

Jamie nodded again. A few people were looking at them for talking so much. Ray knew a lot about things, Jamie had to admit. That's why he didn't mind hanging out with him occasionally. Even if he did like getting into fights. Ray lived somewhere in Essex, quite a long journey getting into London. Maybe that was why he liked to break loose, make the long trip worthwhile.

They listened quietly for a few songs, Jamie watching the performers and how they played their guitars. Could he really do that with a few lessons? Why not? It's not as if he was a simpleton. After all, he had picked up the computer quickly from the few lessons he'd had. Now he had a good job working at Argos in Camden, down in the storeroom: unloading deliveries, logging stock on to the computers, putting things on storage shelves, then sending stuff up in the lift to the shop floor. Always busy, never a dull moment. A job for life. So a guitar should be easy to learn.

He watched all the guitars being taken out of soft and hard cases, machines that glittered under the stage lights. He really wanted to get a guitar now, and learn a few chords. He watched the musicians coming and going. He was fascinated that they just left their guitars lying around while they chatted with their friends or went to the toilet. Surely it would be quite easy to take one.

He nudged Ray and said, 'Let's steal a guitar.'

Ray looked at him and smiled. 'Now you're talking. The thought *had* crossed my mind.'

'Let's keep our eyes open. When one of us sees one left on its own, let's go for it. Forget the drinks, just walk out and grab it.'

'I'm up for that,' Ray said, and the two of them were silent again, looking around the room.

About twenty minutes later Jamie said, 'I see one. Let's go.'

They put their half empty bottles on the bar and nonchalantly walked towards the exit. Everyone was watching a good looking girl up on the stage: long dark hair, singing a Portugese song, something called fado. Kind of mournful. The whole evening was turning into people singing depressing songs. It was a good time to get out.

Just by the exit there was a group of about six people sitting around a table but all of them had their eyes on the stage. Piled right behind them, next to the exit, were at least three guitars. Jamie and Ray walked over to them, and Jamie knelt down and picked the top one up, a soft case, and walked straight out of the door. Ray lagged behind a bit to see if anyone had seen him. No one had. He followed his friend down the stairs and out on to the street.

They walked away quickly, looking behind them. Ducked down a side road and took a roundabout route to get back on to Upper Street.

'So fucking easy,' Ray said eventually. 'They can kiss their axe goodbye.'

Jamie looked at him. 'Was that a joke?'

'Axe is another name for a guitar. Kiss your axe goodbye. Geddit?'

'Got it. Very good.'

Ray said, 'Maybe I should have taken one too. We could become a duo. Ray and Jamie. Or Ramie for short.'

'I think my name should be first. Jamie and Ray. Or Jay for short.'

'Whatever.'

'Now I won't have to buy a guitar,' Jamie said. 'I can start my guitar lessons straight away.'

'Where to next?' Ray said. It was only ten o'clock.

'Let's try The Hope and Anchor,' Jamie said. 'Now that I have a guitar let's see if that barmaid takes more notice of me.'

'That's what I like about you,' Ray said. 'You're always thinking one step ahead.'

Back on Upper Street they were only about one block from The Hope. When they reached the pub they looked through the windows once again. No sign of that black bouncer, but the barmaid was still there, toiling away on the pumps.

'Let's give it a go,' Jamie said. 'What's the worst that can happen?'

'They can throw us out again.'

'Yeah. I can handle that.'

They walked inside and up to the bar. It was pretty packed, rock music coming from a jukebox. Jamie leaned on the bar, the guitar hanging from his shoulder. Eventually the barmaid came over and looked at him.

'Aren't you banned from here?' she asked him, no trace of friendliness at all.

'I don't think so,' Jamie said. 'That was all a misunderstanding. And besides, I'm playing guitar now. I need somewhere to play.'

'We don't have an open mic tonight,' the barmaid said.

'No, but eventually. I want to come back and perform.'

The barmaid looked at the guitar on his back. Jamie could see her mind working. She thought about it long and hard – for about fifteen seconds. Then she said, 'Okay. What would you like?'

'Two pints of Stella please,' Jamie said, handing over a ten pound note. He looked back at Ray and nodded, paid for the drinks and took them away a few paces.

'See what I mean?' he said. 'The guitar did the trick. She looked at it and changed her mind. Without the guitar I don't think she would have served me.'

'Interesting,' Ray said. 'Like that episode of *Curb Your Enthusiasm*.'

Jamie had no idea what he was talking about.

'It's a comedy series,' Ray said. 'About a rich old dude in Los Angeles. In one of the series' he befriends this young black guy and he tells the black guy one day, "If you put on a pair of glasses you'll get more respect from the white man." His theory being that a black man with glasses looks less threatening, more like a professor.'

Jamie still didn't see where this was going.

Ray continued, 'So the black dude buys a pair of glasses and starts walking into posh white establishments with no hassle. People think he's an intellectual. Just like you with your guitar. People will think you're a sensitive soul, a deep thinker.'

'I *am* a deep thinker,' Jamie said. 'But not a sensitive soul. I get you now.'

They stood around a while, finished their pint, then took another drink upstairs to the pool room.

The pool table was taken so they sat and watched.

'We'll stay here until they kick us out,' Jamie said. 'With any luck the barmaid will have to come up and do that herself. I didn't see any bouncers around. Then I'll make my move.'

'What are you going to do? Ask her out?'

'No. I doubt she'd ever go out with me. I just want to get a photo of her on my phone. Something to wank over. Or failing that, a good feel. That will do me.'

'Jesus. You don't mess around,' Ray said. 'Just as well she's old enough.'

'What do you mean?'

'Don't you watch the news? All these old DJs and personalities getting arrested for feeling up young women back in the 60s and 70s. Soon there won't be any famous people left, they'll all be behind bars. Which could be a good thing.'

'Well they shouldn't have picked on young girls should they? Serves them right.'

'Yeah. But what is a young girl anyway? Lots of them dress like they're eighteen when they're only fourteen. It's asking for trouble.'

Jamie couldn't disagree with that. Sometimes women were downright confusing.

Eventually the time ticked past eleven o'clock and they were the only ones left in the pool room. A little while later they heard footsteps coming up the stairs and lo and behold it was the red headed barmaid coming to see them.

She looked at them with surprise and said, 'What are you still doing up here? We're closed.'

Jamie smiled and shrugged. 'We thought you closed at eleven thirty.'

'It's eleven,' the barmaid said. 'Just like everywhere else.'

'Whatever happened to twenty-four hour opening?' Ray asked.

'It didn't catch on,' the barmaid said. 'A complete waste of time. Now drink up. It's time to leave.'

Jamie and Ray stood up and emptied their glasses. 'What's your name anyway?' Jamie asked.

'Gill,' the barmaid said. 'Gill with a G.'

'Gill,' Jamie said, savouring the word. 'Can I be your G man Gill?'

Gill shook her head. 'No you can't. I've already got a boyfriend.'

'Lucky man,' Ray said. 'Can we at least have a feel of your titties?'

Jamie looked at his friend with amazement. He felt like laughing. Or running. He didn't know what the hell would happen next. Gill was looking at them, blushing. He looked at her breasts in her light blue T-shirt. Her chest was going up and down, heavy breathing. Probably from being annoyed, Jamie thought.

Then, quick as a flash, Ray was right in front of her and trying to pull up her T-shirt. Jamie couldn't believe it, the two of them struggling as Ray pulled up and Gill pulled down. Then the T-shirt ripped, and Ray ripped it some more, until Gill was standing there in her bra, the two sides of the T-shirt hanging from her shoulders.

'Wow,' Ray said. 'Get a load of that.'

Gill slapped Ray hard across the face, then Jamie joined his friend and both of them were on her, pushing Gill back across the pool table and lifting up her bra. Her breasts sprang loose and wobbled around in front of them. Both of them had a good feel, Jamie hardly believing that this was happening. Gill was struggling and swearing at them and eventually Jamie said, 'Let's go Ray.' He didn't want to lose his job at Argos over a bit of free tit.

Ray looked at him with disappointment, clearly wanting to go a bit further. Jamie picked up his new guitar and headed for the stairs. Ray reluctantly followed, leaving Gill half on the pool table looking at them with hatred. They went down the stairs and over to the side door. The keys were sitting in the lock so they opened it and went out. There was no sign of any other staff around.

## CHAPTER EIGHT.

'It must be tough,' Scobie said. 'Realising that you'll never work again. Either as a criminal or in the straight world.'

'It is,' Glenn said, taking a sip of his pint. 'And what's worse is knowing that you could do a better job than most people given the chance.'

'Why don't you become a taxi driver? They don't ask too many questions.'

'You must be joking. No way would they let an ex-con become a taxi driver. They'd think I was going to rape every single woman customer. And with all due respect, I'd get bored out of my mind sitting around in a car all day waiting for fares. And I can't afford to buy a car anyway.'

'I just rent mine,' Scobie said. 'Never bought one in my life.'

'And how many hours do you have to work before you pay off the weekly rent?'

'About seventy,' Scobie laughed. 'But I can work when I want. And come in here afterwards.'

The Home Cottage was fairly full, a weekday lunchtime: postal workers, office workers, and travelling salesmen. When Glenn had been in his teens the pub had been run by a very old woman. It had been quite rough in those days, even had sawdust on the floor if he remembered correctly, but it had character. After several re-fits over the years it now looked pretty much like any other kind of pub, and served the same kind of food as well. Glenn preferred the old days when all they sold were cheese and onion rolls. There was something about a cheese and onion roll and a pint of Young's that went down just fine.

'I apply for jobs occasionally,' Glenn said. 'When I get the urge. But everything is so Internet based these days I find it all baffling. I'm like an old gunslinger being left behind by the times. I only apply for jobs where I can ring someone up and talk to a real person. Fucked if I'm going to fill in any application forms online. I don't even have the Internet at home or even a computer.'

Scobie nodded sympathetically. 'And because of all these Euro people coming in, you need so many bits of paper these days. Even to drive a van you need qualifications. And no one believes you're British anymore. Have to take your passport with you, proof of address etc, to every minor job interview. What a pain. I may work long hours but I'm thankful.'

Glenn nodded. 'And it keeps you away from your wife too.'

Scobie smiled. 'Yes, that's a big plus.'

Glenn had seen Scobie's wife once when she came to haul him out of the pub after he'd been in there all day. She was as fat as Scobie but had enough stamina to bawl him out in front of everyone, creating an embarrassing scene. Then she'd led him out of the pub by his ear, Glenn sitting there looking at her thinking, how the hell would you find the hole amongst all that flesh?

Glenn preferred slim women; he just couldn't go with a fat woman at all. Not that he'd been with any kind of a woman for a while, about three years if you discounted a London prostitute, taken one drunken night in Soho last year, an experience he'd regretted ever since. Yes slim women were preferable, even if they were ugly in the face. Then you just turned them over and thought about someone else. But with a fat woman you couldn't even do that. Because of all the fat. May as well stick your dick in a tub of lard.

Glenn was on his third pint now, the clock ticking around towards three o'clock. He wanted a whisky for the road and then he'd shove off home. Spend Friday evening alone as usual, see if there was anything decent on TV. Chance would be a fine thing. Maybe there would be a decent film on one of the lesser known channels, a Van Damme or a Seagal, something with lots of action so he wouldn't have to think too much.

Scobie bought him a whisky and they had a couple of games of darts, Glenn winning once again. He often wondered, if he had his youth again, whether he could have become a professional darts player. He very rarely got beaten, and if he'd put his mind to it all those years ago, when darts was becoming really popular and getting on TV, maybe he could have made the grade. But it was too late now. He wouldn't have the stamina at his age, and all the top players were in their twenties and thirties.

He went for a final piss, didn't bother washing his hands after, shook Scobie's hand and left the pub.

The walk home took him twenty minutes. It was a warm summer's day and he enjoyed looking at all the young women strolling around wearing virtually nothing. What he would give for a quick roll in the hay with one of them. Was that too much to ask? He could die happy then, he was certain.

When he arrived home his mood dipped when he heard the sound of Daisy up in her first floor kitchen. She had the radio on, Capitol Gold, and was singing out of tune to 'Good Vibrations' by The Beach Boys. Glenn looked on the hall table to see if he had any mail. Now and again something arrived for him, usually a letter from the council complaining that he hadn't done something. Or the Job Centre asking him to go in for a progress chat. Thankfully there was nothing.

He walked slowly up the stairs, hoping to get past the kitchen without any Daisy interaction, but there she was at the sink and she turned around and saw him.

'How are you Glenn?' she said, slurring her words, obviously on the medication again.

'Fine', Glenn said, hoping to just walk on by. But Daisy came over and looked at him, staring as if she was trying to look deep into his soul. She'd done this a few times before and it unnerved him. She was weaving a bit, unsteady on her feet, her face bright red from whatever she'd been taking, either pills or alcohol. She was dressed in a flowery summer dress, bright red fluffy slippers on her feet. Her dark hair looked freshly washed, frizzy and un-brushed, coming down to her shoulders.

Glenn turned and stepped up the couple of stairs to the next level where Daisy and Vernon's bedroom and living room were.

'Glenn?' Daisy said behind him.

He turned around and was amazed to see her standing there holding up her skirt to her waist - and she had no knickers on at all. Her dark triangle of hair was looking straight back at him, a sight he hadn't seen for a while – the London prostitute had shaved all of hers off.

'See anything you like?' Daisy slurred.

Glenn stood and looked. There was no harm in looking after all. 'Not bad,' he said.

'Why don't you come here and touch it?' Daisy said.

Glenn thought about it for maybe half a minute. It might be a nice idea to run his fingers through that bush. Daisy had a pretty good figure on her; it was just her face that ruined the look, always puffed up from the drugs. And that slurry voice too.

Glenn thought *to hell with it*, and walked back down the few steps to the kitchen doorway. He put his right hand down and stroked the bush that was waiting for him. He did it slowly feeling himself getting hard. Daisy closed her eyes and urged him on, making quiet moaning sounds.

Glenn reached down a little further and slipped a finger underneath her. A few rubs and he could feel her starting to get wet. She opened her legs slightly so he could get two fingers down there.

'That's nice,' she said. 'Vernon's not back for another hour.'

Glenn unzipped his trousers and released his cock that was straining to get out. He took her right hand and put it down there, moved her hand, showing her what to do. But she was so out of her head on meds she didn't really have any coordination.

Glenn pushed her back into the kitchen and walked her over to the kitchen table. He nudged her down slowly towards the table so she was bending over it. Then he lifted up her dress and looked at her arse.

It was a pretty nice arse he had to admit. Much better than could be expected. With her dress around her waist he started working his fingers some more until she was nice and wet. Then he stood behind her and gently eased his cock inside.

The feeling of heat and warmth and wet took over, and he started to slide in and out slowly. Daisy was moaning and offering encouragement, her head bowed down on the table, God knows what thoughts going on in her head. Did she really know what she was doing, strung out on medication? Glenn had to admit, that no matter how rough the woman might be, as soon as he was inside her, it all felt the same, all felt as good as he remembered. He could block out all other thoughts and worries and lose himself inside the passion. He started moving to 'Maggie May' which was now on the radio.

He kept going for about five minutes and then started thinking about Vernon coming home, Vernon the mechanic or whatever he was, with his strong arms. Short little fucker looked like that actor Robert Duvall when he was in his thirties. Could give Glenn a whole load of physical trouble if he wanted to. Glenn thought he'd better finish what he'd started.

He wound himself up for the big finish, telling Daisy he was about to come, and then shot off inside her, not even bothering to ask whether she was on the pill or not. He figured that with all the drugs she was taking her insides were probably all shot to hell anyway. And it felt so good to let it all off inside her, probably the best feeling in the world, though he'd never taken heroin, maybe that would beat it. He pulled out his cock and shoved it with difficulty back inside his jeans. Then he pulled down Daisy's dress and gave her a pat on the backside. She remained over the table though, still out of breath, trying to recover.

He moved her gently and sat her down on one of the two wooden kitchen chairs. She looked up at him with a smile, totally zoned out. Glenn walked to the sink and filled a glass with water and took it back to her. He held it to her mouth and forced a few sips down her throat.

Then he heard the front door opening downstairs and Vernon calling up, 'Only me!'

That was a fucking short hour Glenn thought.

He left the kitchen quickly and just made it round the corner to his flight of stairs as Vernon went up and into the kitchen. Glenn had to creep quietly up the rest of the stairs and heard Vernon saying something to his wife. Glenn crept into the bathroom and closed the door and locked it.

He unzipped himself and had a long piss, Daisy's juices still damp on his dick and pubes. He stood at the sink afterwards and washed himself down with soap and water, dried himself on the old hand towel that was always there. He didn't know who it belonged to. He flushed the toilet, opened the door, and Vernon was standing right there on the landing in front of him.

'Jesus!' Glenn said. 'You nearly gave me a heart attack.'

'Sorry,' Vernon said, one of the most polite men you could wish to meet. 'Need to take a leak. Had a few beers after work.'

'Yeah, me too,' Glenn said. 'But not after work.'

He squeezed past Vernon and waited until the bathroom door was shut before putting his keys quietly into his bedroom door and stepping in. Once inside he let out a deep breath and slumped on to the bed.

He thought about Daisy and the events that had just taken place. One of the nice surprises that happened occasionally in life. He had to admit he'd enjoyed it a lot. He wondered if Daisy would be willing to do it again sometime or whether he should quit while he was ahead. If they carried on she might want him to kiss her and he wasn't too sure if he wanted to do that. But bending over the kitchen table, he could get into that again.

He could feel himself getting hard once more. Not bad for a fifty-eight year old. There was life in the old dog yet.

## *CHAPTER NINE.*

A few days after meeting Sara Shriver and walking her back to her house, Jason dropped one of his CDs through her letterbox. It was a 'best of' collection of ten songs from his two recorded CDs, songs that he thought would be suitable for her to cover. Surely she would like one of them he thought. It took her two weeks to get in touch.

He was sitting in his flat fiddling away on his guitar when his mobile rang.

'Hi Jason, it's Sara. I really like your songs. Why don't we meet up sometime?'

Jason looked in his diary, and now a few days later, he was walking the short distance to her house, his Martin guitar slung over his shoulder in its soft case. He felt a little nervous. He was going to a film star's house! He wondered if there would be servants or PR people or other hangers on. Probably not. This was Chiswick after all, not Hollywood.

He opened her front gate and walked through the small front garden; neat lawn and flower beds. He wondered if Sara did the gardening. He couldn't imagine it. She'd probably get pestered by passers-by or overly friendly neighbours. He rang the doorbell and waited.

Sara opened the door wearing jeans, cowboy boots, and a dark green blouse. She gave him a big smile and ushered him in. Jason wondered whether to shake her hand or give one of those fake

Hollywood air-kisses, but opted to just do nothing at all.

'Welcome to my humble abode,' Sara said. 'I hope you weren't expecting a Hollywood house.'

'Not at all,' Jason said. 'We're not in Hollywood.'

'Yes, thank goodness for that. People always expect me to be a millionaire.'

The house looked pretty similar to Jason's. A large Victorian, except this one wasn't divided into flats. Probably had three floors in total. He followed her down the hallway, studying her figure as he hadn't had the opportunity the first time they'd met. Her legs were thinner than he'd imagined, a nice slim build. Classy. Probably about five-nine in her stocking feet.

They turned right into a living room and inside there was a man sitting on a chair with a guitar. He looked to be in his mid-thirties, short hair, clean shaven. He put down his instrument and stood up and now Jason could see he was about six feet one, with broad shoulders and an athletic physique, unusual for a musician. Sara introduced him as Rick and they shook hands, the big man almost crushing Jason's hand with his strength. The guy looked like an American marine rather than a guitar player. He had an English accent though.

'Rick's the leader of my band,' Sara said. 'He does all the arrangements.'

'Great,' Jason said, a little disappointed that he wouldn't be on his own with Sara. But then again, why should she want to be alone with him? She hardly knew him. He might be a celebrity stalker or something.

'Would you like a cup of tea?' Sara asked. 'Or water? Or something stronger?'

'Water will be fine,' Jason said. He sat down on the sofa while Sara left the room.

'I really like your songs,' Rick said. 'I'm sure we can use a couple on our next CD. We just have to sort out which ones.'

'That's great,' Jason said. 'I left off my more personal songs, just put on the ones that other people could sing.'

Rick nodded. 'Have you got many more?'

'About a hundred and fifty, though most of them I would only perform for myself.'

'Wow. Prolific.'

'Not really. I've been writing since I was sixteen, so if you work out the average it's only about four songs a year.'

'Still. It's more than most.'

'I guess,' Jason said. 'I think I'm slowing down in my old age though. I have enough for about four good albums. What's the point in writing more? Most singers perform the same twenty songs their whole career.'

Rick nodded. 'You know what they say about most singer-songwriters.'

'What's that?'

'Their first two albums are always the best and then it's all downhill after that.'

'In most cases that's true,' Jason said. 'Except for people like Dylan and Springsteen, and Neil Young. And Leonard Cohen.'

'Yes. People like that never run out of ideas.'

'And probably a few more. Steve Earle,' Jason said.

'Paul Simon,' Rick said.

Jason nodded. 'Gordon Lightfoot.'

'Guy Clark.'

'Townes Van Zandt.'

'Jackson Browne.'

'Warren Zevon.'

'Kris Kristofferson.'

'Tom Petty.'

'Nick Lowe.'

'John Stewart.'

'John Stewart? What did he do?' Rick asked.

'Well his most famous song is 'Daydream Believer', The Monkees hit, but he wrote a whole lot more than that. The guy was prolific. I have about eight of his CDs and I like them all. He's been one of my favourites for years. Died in 2006 I think.'

'I'll have to check him out on Spotify,' Rick said.

'You won't be disappointed. His best albums are *Cannons in the Rain*, *Wingless Angels*, and *Bombs Away Dream Babies*.'

Rick picked up a pen and asked Jason to repeat the titles. '*Bombs Away Dream Babies*? What's that meant to mean?'

'I haven't a clue,' Jason said. 'But it's a cool title.'

They were silent for a few seconds as Rick continued writing. 'So you've done a bit of touring in the past?' he said when he'd finished.

Jason filled him in on his previous tours, Rick nodding his head and knowing all the names that Jason mentioned, even Calista Shaw.

'Impressive,' he said. 'My only tours have been in bands that no one's heard of. Made a couple of CDs that no one's heard of either.'

'How did you meet Sara?' Jason asked.

'Through a friend of a friend. I also live in Chiswick so that makes it easy.'

Sara returned with a glass of water and handed it to Jason.

'Right,' Rick said. 'Let's form a circle and get tuned up.'

They set up three chairs and sat down facing each other. Jason took out his Martin, while Rick sat down with a Taylor, and Sara with a black Takamine. It didn't take long to tune up as they were all basically in the right area already. Sara had a big smile on her face, obviously enjoying the occasion.

Rick picked up Jason's CD from the floor and looked at the track listing. 'The two we'd really like to hear first are 'One Guitar' and 'Whisky Lingers'.'

'A good choice,' Jason said. 'I've brought some lyric and chord sheets with me.' From the zippered pouch on his case he brought out sheets of typed lyrics with chords for all ten songs on his CD. He handed them over to Rick. 'Sorry, I only brought one copy of each.'

'No problem,' Sara said. 'We have the technology to reproduce. Give them to me.'

Jason handed them over and she left the room again.

'Photocopier,' Rick said. 'Film stars have everything.'

In a few minutes Sara was back carrying extra copies of all the songs. She brought a small table over and set it down in front of them.

Jason was pleased with their choices; two songs he'd always thought were good enough to be on someone else's album. He put his capo on the second fret for 'One Guitar' and started flat picking in a country style. When he started singing the first verse though he found that his voice was a little shaky. He'd never sung in front of a film star before. But on the second verse Rick started to pick out some lead guitar and Jason relaxed. He glanced up at Sara who was sitting there smiling at them both, watching the chords he was playing. On the second chorus she joined in with the singing, and Jason relaxed even more. He was pleased that she knew the tune already. She'd obviously been listening to his CD quite a few times in the last two weeks.

On the final chorus all three of them joined in, and the harmonies sounded good. Jason very rarely sang or played with other people - he didn't like rehearsing much - and it was nice to have a couple of people who could pick things up quickly. When the song ended they all smiled and congratulated each other and Rick said, 'That's a definite possibility. Simple but effective.'

'Great song!' Sara said.

'It sounds a lot better with other people on it,' Jason said. 'Almost like a real record.'

Rick nodded. 'A few extra instruments make all the difference. Wait until we get some bass on it. Maybe some drums.'

'Or a fiddle,' Jason said. 'I always like a little fiddle.'

Sara laughed.

'Don't we all,' Rick said, looking sideways at Sara.

Jason laughed as well. Things were going swimmingly.

For the next song 'Whisky Lingers', he did a bit of finger-picking and Rick once again provided lead. On the chorus it was just Sara singing with him. Jason looked over at her, wishing his friends could see him now. Not that he had that many friends. He still couldn't believe this was happening. Sara still hadn't played her guitar though. He presumed she was just a basic rhythm player.

When the song finished Rick said, 'Once again, a very good song. Have you got any other CDs? I'd like to listen to some more.'

'Sure,' Jason said. 'Would you like me to drop another one off?'

'Yes, just drop it through Sara's letterbox sometime. No big hurry. We've only just started putting things together for the next CD.'

'Maybe you could do a whole CD of Jason Campbell songs,' Jason joked. Then added, 'Just one of my cowboy dreams.'

Rick nodded. 'Like Waylon Jennings doing a whole album of Billy Joe Shaver?'

Jason was amazed that Rick had heard of Billy Joe Shaver, one of the greatest and yet least known country songwriters. 'Sort of,' he said. 'Though I wouldn't claim to be in his league.'

'Billy Joe is great,' Sara said. 'We were wanting to do 'Live Forever' on the CD. We do it in our live shows and it always goes down well.'

'It's a great song,' Jason said. 'Why don't we do it now. I'd like to see you play.'

'Okay,' Sara said, seemingly glad to join in fully at last.

She put her capo on and Rick told her to start off. She started finger-picking in a quiet and basic way and Rick picked along with her giving it some extra confidence. Then Sara started singing the song that Jason knew so well - because he owned the Billy Joe Shaver CD that it appeared on. It had also been featured briefly in the recent Jeff Bridges film *Crazy Heart*, a film that Jason liked well enough to see twice. The first time he'd seen it had been with a casual girlfriend of his called Jane, who had dumped him for good several weeks later because of his ambivalent attitude towards their relationship. She had called him Lazy Heart as she'd stomped out of the door, a moniker that Jason thought fit him pretty well – after all, he had never once got close to marrying anyone, so he probably was a bit lazy in that department. He'd then gone to see the film a second time on his own, being able to enjoy it much more without Jane by his side. He'd been meaning to write a song called 'Lazy Heart' ever since but still hadn't got around to it.

When the chorus came around Jason joined in with the two of them and sang harmony. He had always been able to sing harmony easily, probably due to singing along to Beatles songs in his youth. The song was very short and was over within three minutes. They congratulated each other afterwards.

'That sounded great,' Sara said. 'Maybe you could do some vocals on our CD too.'

Jason blushed. 'That would be fun.' Things were getting better by the minute.

'Let's try another couple of yours,' Rick said, picking Jason's CD off the floor once again and looking at the cover. 'This one intrigues me. 'Chameleon Ways'. Tell me how you came to write that one.'

Jason told them the story of Teddy Peppers and how he'd written a song about it afterwards, turning it into a kind of wild-west country song that he always thought Johnny Cash could have sung if he was still alive.

'You're right,' Rick said. 'It would have been perfect for Cash on his American Recordings.'

Jason nodded. It was one of his biggest regrets that Johnny Cash had never recorded or even heard any of his songs. But why would he? Jason was unknown and didn't have any links to Nashville.

He strummed the intro to 'Chameleon Ways' and Rick followed him on lead.

And so it went on.

\*\*\*

On the walk home afterwards, Jason couldn't believe his luck. He'd been with Sara and Rick about three hours in total and they'd sung loads of songs together, a few of Sara's as well, which Jason had thought were a little weak, but nodded as if he'd liked them. Then Rick did one of his own, an up tempo song about war called 'This Band is My Band' which was quite impressive, but too dark to go on Sara's CD. Rick had been in the army in his early twenties, and had fought in the Iraq War in 2003. Now he worked as a musician and bit part actor, and also from home doing something computer related that Jason didn't understand. They'd both given him their mobile numbers and emails, and then had a glass of wine together in the large kitchen, along with some olives and crisps. This is the life Jason had thought. *The life I've been waiting for.*

He stopped in a corner shop on the way home and bought some wine and bits of food for himself. Things were looking up. He would have liked to just go home and drink a few glasses and play some more, but he remembered he still had a couple of evening lessons to do. His work was never done. He left the corner shop and carried on home.

# CHAPTER TEN.

The next morning Jason received a phone call at eleven. He picked it up and his heart sank when he heard it was Jamie the troublemaker on the other end. After saying hello Jamie said, 'I've got myself a guitar and I need some lessons.'

Jason was regretting giving the guy his business card the last time he'd seen him.

'Can you see me today?' Jamie added. 'I'll come to where you live.'

Jason picked up his diary and looked at his schedule. Not too much on. 'I can fit you in at two. How would that be?'

'Fine. How much does it cost?'

'Twenty pounds an hour,' Jason said.

'Phew. Expensive.'

'Well, you'll leave here with a lot of ideas and a lot of homework. It'll be worth it.'

'Okay. Tell me how to get there.'

Jason told him which tubes to take from Camden and said he'd meet him at Turnham Green station at half-one. Then he rang off.

Jason showered and dressed, took another lesson at twelve, then had a sandwich for lunch. At one fifteen he left his flat for the walk to the station. He often met pupils there. It was easier than giving directions and ensured they turned up on time. There was nothing worse than someone turning up half an hour late and having lessons overlap. It was just too stressful.

Jamie arrived on time, his guitar slung over his shoulder in its case. They shook hands and Jason led the way to Highsmith Road.

'It's quite a way from Camden,' Jamie said. 'I don't think I'll be doing this every week.'

Jason was relieved to hear that. 'Come once a month then. That'll give you time to work on stuff. Or maybe you'll just lose interest.'

'I had a look on You Tube the other day,' Jamie said. 'So many guitar lessons on that. It's a wonder anyone needs you anymore.'

'That's true. I've looked at a few things on there myself. Soon enough the Internet will kill everything.' Jason was amazed how many guitar tutors were on You Tube, hundreds of them. And why did they do it exactly? Just to see how many hits they could get? They were putting a lot of people out of business. He'd thought of putting himself on there as a way of getting new pupils but he didn't have a proper camera and couldn't be bothered with it all anyway. There were too many people in this world desperate to put themselves on the 'net. He'd leave it to the younger generation.

As they walked up Fareham, Jason couldn't resist his latest story. 'Yesterday I was singing songs to a film actress who lives in this road,' he said. 'She's thinking of putting a couple of my songs on her next CD.'

'Yeah? A film actress that sings? Is it Gwyneth Paltrow?'

Jason laughed. 'No it's not.' He was amazed that Jamie knew that Gwyneth Paltrow also sang.

Jamie said, 'I saw that country film she was in recently. It was rubbish. She was pretty good though. Nice legs.'

'*Country Strong* I think it was called,' Jason said. 'I didn't see it. I remember her as a karaoke singer in a film called *Duets*. She was good in that. She sang 'Bette Davis Eyes'.'

'I'll look out for it. So who's this film star you were with?'

'She's called Sara Shriver. She's currently in that ITV series *Prince and Langer*. She's done a lot of films over the years, even one with Burt Reynolds.'

'And she's recording CDs now?'

'Yes, and she has her own band. Does a bit of touring as well.'

'Can we go and say hello? I've never met a film star before.'

Jason cringed at the thought. 'No we can't. She likes her privacy. And I've only met her a couple of times. She's not my best buddy yet. I won't even show you where she lives. I don't trust you.'

Jamie looked a little hurt. 'Just because I caused a fight in the pub once?'

'That might have something to do with it. I hardly know you. You might turn out to be a celebrity stalker. Anyway, you don't need to know where she lives. She lives in this road though. I'll tell you that much.'

Jamie started looking around them as they walked, trying to pick out the film star's home. 'They all look the same,' he said.

'What do you expect? A swimming pool in the front garden?'

'At least. Or maybe a fancy motor.'

'That's a good point,' Jason said. 'I have no idea what car she drives or even if she drives. I've seen her on the Underground.'

'She goes on the tube? She can't be that famous then.'

Jason had to agree with that. Someone like Gwyneth Paltrow wouldn't go on the tube. But Sara was more famous in the US than England, though her TV series was pretty popular.

They came to the end of Fareham and were soon walking down Willeford Road. When they came to Jason's house Jamie nodded with approval.

'Nice,' he said. 'Is the whole thing yours?'

'No. It's divided into four flats.'

'A pity.'

Inside the flat Jason made them both a cup of tea and handed out some biscuits. Jamie unzipped his guitar case and brought out a dark red guitar with a shiny finish. It was a snazzy looking Yamaha electro-acoustic, probably the kind a girl would have. Jason would never play a red guitar. You had to have standards.

'Nice,' he lied. 'Where did you get it?'

'In Islington,' Jamie said. 'Cost me a hundred quid.'

Jason nodded. 'That sounds about right. Do you know any chords yet?'

'I don't know shit. That's why I'm here.'

Jason took Jamie's guitar and strummed it. It was badly out of tune. They sat down on a couple of chairs facing each other and Jason tuned it, using his old Epiphone guitar that was lying there on the floor to compare it with. Then he handed it to Jamie.

'I'll give you a sheet of paper telling you how to tune it yourself,' he said. 'Or just look on You Tube. There are plenty of guys on there telling you how to do it.'

'Okay boss,' Jamie nodded.

'Now I'll teach you three chords so you can play 'I Fought the Law'. Okay?'

'Fine. That's the song I like.'

'And if you forget the tune just Google it. Plenty of people have recorded it over the years.'

Jamie nodded. 'Take it away maestro.'

\*\*\*

One hour later, almost on the dot, Jamie was walking away from Jason's and back to the station. He was £20 worse off. He had tried walking out without paying, but Jason had stopped him at the front door and said, 'Aren't you forgetting something?' Jamie had reluctantly handed over the money, hoping he'd get that first lesson for free seeing how he and Jason were now almost friends. Or were they? He was a hard guy to read, acting professional throughout the lesson, not really laughing at Jamie's attempts at humour.

Jamie wondered if he'd ever come out here again. It was a long way to come just for a guitar lesson. Maybe he'd find someone in Camden instead. Jason had taught him a few chords and also how to strum. Jamie had found it all a bit confusing though and wondered whether he was really cut out to be a guitar man. He'd left with about three sheets of paper stuck into his case, stuff he had to learn before his next visit, if he ever came. Three sheets of paper for twenty quid. He could see who was getting the better deal out of it.

A few minutes later he was on Fareham Road and once again he started looking around for the film star's house. He would like to meet her one day that was for sure. He would look her up on the Internet when he got home, see if he recognised her. Sara Shriver. Also see if there were any nude photos of her. There usually were. Most actresses were willing to strip at the drop of a hat. Or at the drop of a few bucks. And he'd also noticed on the Internet recently a whole load of fake nude photos of famous women. People would take a photo of an actress's head and stick it on a nude porno photo of someone else. Some of the results looked quite realistic. Jamie had been fooled at first, thinking the photos were real, but then found there were so many of them, and some of them were downright ridiculous, that he had figured them out as fakes. He wondered why the film stars didn't get their legal team on to it, get someone to take the photos off. Maybe they just liked their naked selves on the world wide web. Any publicity was good publicity after all. Or was it?

He thought about the incident with the barmaid Gill a few weeks ago. Jason hadn't mentioned it so presumably he hadn't heard about it. That was just as well. If Jason had known he probably wouldn't have accepted him for a lesson, so going for a lesson was also a good way of finding out just who Gill had told. Jamie felt a bit bad about it now, but it had been worth it just to see her tits and get a quick feel. He wished he'd taken a photo on his smart phone, but the memory was still fresh in his mind and had been vivid enough to jerk off to a few times at home. He still fantasised about Gill, would love to get her in the sack for real. But that would never happen now. Thanks to Ray. What a crazy fucker he was turning out to be. Who'd have thunk it? An IT worker who turned into a raving loony after a few drinks. Jamie wondered if he should hang out with him anymore. He might turn out to be a liability and he didn't want to get into trouble now that his life was firmly on track at Argos.

He looked at his watch. Still most of the day left. On Sunday he would be going down to Redgate, his old home town, to see his father. They spoke about once a fortnight on the phone and Jamie went down to see him occasionally. His father lived in a crummy bed-sit thanks to his criminal past, so they usually met in the Home Cottage as it was just a hundred yards from the train station. His father drank too much and was full of crazy ideas about how he was going to change his life around. Nothing ever came of them though; he would just sit there in the pub downing more and more drink. Then, if it was a nice day, they'd go for a walk through the town centre and end up in some burger bar eating crap food for another hour. As if Sundays weren't depressing enough. Maybe he should take Ray down to meet his father sometime, tell him 'this is the way you'll end up if you don't start behaving yourself.' It might help to change his crazy ways.

As he neared Turnham Green tube Jamie saw a woman walking towards him with a guitar slung over her shoulder. She was a good looking blonde in her twenties. As they passed each other she looked at him and smiled. Fucking A! Jamie thought. This guitar image really works! Maybe he should just walk around with one on his back all the time, didn't really matter if he learned to play it or not.

He wondered if he should tell his dad about his new hobby. No. He would keep it secret for the moment. His dad would just poo-poo the idea, that was for sure. That was the story of his life, getting put down by his parents. Not that he ever saw his mother anymore. She had disappeared many years ago. The last he'd heard she was living up north near Newcastle with a loser of an electrician. Jamie's last brief phone call with her had been about three years ago. 'I'm living with an electrician, he turns me on,' his mother had said, expecting him to laugh at her joke. Then she'd added, 'He's very good in the horizontal position.' Jamie had almost puked. The thought of his mother having sex was just too awful to laugh at. With any luck the electrician would electrocute her one day.

Jamie walked up to the ticket barrier, swiped his Oyster and went through. He'd told his mother to get a new scriptwriter and hadn't spoken to her since.

## *CHAPTER ELEVEN.*

The day after his brief sexual encounter with Daisy, Glenn woke up with an uncomfortable feeling in his stomach; it was a mixture of a little guilt with more than a little dread.

How would he be able to face Daisy again, and how would he be able to walk out of the house without being seen? And worse than that, it was the weekend and Vernon would be around. How would he be able to face the Robert Duvall look-alike without betraying something on his face? But then again, that could work in his favour. If Vernon was around then Daisy couldn't confront him. She would be under Vernon's eagle eye with no escape route for her.

Glenn scrambled out of bed and looked in his food cupboard. Did he have enough there for the weekend? He thought not. That would mean a trip to the corner store, usually a simple operation but now requiring the planning of a military coup.

He looked down at his pyjamas and noticed his penis was starting to rise. It was the thought of Daisy and their session yesterday. He wondered how she was feeling this morning. Maybe she was so zoned out on drugs she just wouldn't remember any of it. Maybe it would all be like a dream. A wet dream. Did women even have them? He supposed they did.

He made himself breakfast of tea and toast and marmalade and sat down in his armchair. He didn't even like marmalade that much and yet he ate it nearly every day. Why was that? Force of habit? What else was there to eat for breakfast, surely the most pointless meal of the day.

He turned on his 12" analogue TV. He couldn't afford digital TV and he'd heard from a few people that it was crap. They'd told him that you couldn't hear dialogue any more and had to use subtitles. So Glenn had bought a Freeview set-top box for £20 to convert his old TV when the digital switch had happened. He could hear dialogue perfectly as the sound on analogue was so much better. And the picture was great too. Only problem was, with so many Freeview channels most of it was shit. Just like American TV. It had been simpler when he was a child. Just three channels then.

He switched to Channel 4 to watch the morning horse racing show. He wasn't a betting man but he didn't mind watching it. It was a whole lot better than watching *Saturday Morning Kitchen* on BBC 1, that James Martin guy who seemed to be on TV every time he turned it on. Some people were just workaholics. The guy must be loaded. And he was getting fatter by the week, all that food he no doubt ate right after he cooked it. Glenn took a bite of his crunchy toast.

There was a faint knock on his door. He looked over wondering who it could be. Maybe it was Vernon come to beat his head in. He wondered whether he should answer or just ignore it. The faint tapping came again.

Glenn got to his feet, walked over to the door and opened it. Daisy was standing there in a nightdress. Glenn was just about to say something when Daisy held her finger to her lips telling him to be quiet. Then she came into his room and closed the door behind her.

Daisy still held her finger to her lips as she stepped up close and reached down towards his prick. She started rubbing him there and it didn't take much for it to rise to the occasion. Glenn wanted to ask her where Vernon was but as talking was not aloud he couldn't. Then Daisy's face came towards him and she started kissing him on the cheek and then the lips. Glenn couldn't believe this was happening but as he grew harder all rational thought was starting to leave his head.

Daisy let go of him after about a minute and then turned towards the bed and leaned over it. She reached around and pulled up her nightdress and once again she wasn't wearing any underwear. Glenn dropped his pyjamas and started rubbing his cock along the crack of her bum and then he slipped easily inside her. She was soaking wet and he hadn't even touched her down there. It reminded him of a girl at school, one of the first times he'd ever touched pussy, who'd been sopping wet at the touch of his hand, so wet he couldn't believe it. He thought about his old school girlfriend as he pumped away and within a few minutes he was once again shooting off inside Daisy, both of them trying to keep quiet because no doubt about it, Vernon was downstairs somewhere within earshot.

Struggling for breath, Glenn withdrew his member and pulled his pyjamas back up. Daisy was still leaning over the bed trying to get her breath back. He pulled her nightdress back over her bum and lifted her by the shoulders, then guided her towards the door. He opened it quietly, looked to make sure the coast was clear, then motioned Daisy towards the bathroom. She disappeared inside and shut the door.

Glenn closed his door and slumped down in his armchair, wondering what the hell was going on. He couldn't keep this up everyday and get away with it. Vernon was bound to figure it out eventually even if he wasn't too bright. Glenn stood up and quickly put on a pair of jeans, then a jumper over his pyjama top, and a pair of trainers without any socks. He grabbed some money and left his room without locking it.

Down on the first floor he saw Vernon in the kitchen sitting at the table reading a tabloid newspaper. The radio was on. Glenn said hello and carried on walking. At least Vernon hadn't been sitting underneath his room when he'd been pumping Daisy. The kitchen was on the opposite side of the house so hearing something would have been difficult. Plus the radio would have drowned out any noise as well.

In the small corner store twenty yards from his lodgings, Glenn bought enough food for the weekend. Most of the food in there was canned, which was fine by him. He wasn't much of a cook, or even a James Martin, and didn't believe in the theory that fruit and veg made you healthier and live longer. What was the point in him living longer anyway? He had nothing much to live for. Or maybe he would have to rethink that philosophy now that Daisy was putting herself forward as his new woman. He bought cans of beans and corned beef, bread and milk, and several cans of pasta sauce. He knew how to cook pasta anyway, and pouring sauce all over it was an easy meal. He also bought some cans of beer, and two cheap bottles of red wine. He felt he deserved a treat after getting laid twice in the space of two days. He wondered if Daisy would visit his room tomorrow. Probably not. It was Sunday, a day of rest.

'Stocking up?' July asked him.

July ran the store with his mother and they lived together in the house attached to the shop; a forty year old man whose life was going nowhere. He had short curly hair and crooked teeth and was always tanned. Glenn imagined he sat in his back garden whenever his mother was on the till. He certainly never seemed to go abroad. Glenn had asked him once how he came to be called July and his explanation had been, 'That's the month I was born in.' And had then added, 'It's also the name of a character in *Lonesome Dove*, a western mini-series on TV a while ago.' Glenn remembered the series vaguely, but reckoned it had been made in the

1980s, so therefore July couldn't have been named after the character as he would have been born sometime in the 1970s. He reckoned July was just instilling some kind of romanticism into his stupid name. Glenn had then thought about other people being named after the month they were born in. Like April or May or June. It was okay if you were a woman. Even January was a woman's name wasn't it? And August was probably a name too. Glenn was just glad he wasn't named February, the month *he'd* been born in. He'd be Feb for short. Something a bit gay about that.

'Yeah,' Glenn said. 'Can't see me going out this weekend. Bunkering in.'

'Nothing much to do around here anyway,' July said.

Glenn nodded. Except shag my neighbour's wife he felt like saying. 'It'll be sport on the radio for me,' he said.

'Me too,' July said. 'What a life.'

'Don't worry. It'll all be over before you know it.'

'With any luck.' July half smiled at him.

Glenn had never heard July say anything remotely philosophical or personal before. He thought he'd better leave the shop before July started telling him all about his problems. He picked up his two carrier bags, said goodbye, and left quickly.

\*\*\*

Now it was Sunday, one week later, and Glenn was sitting in the Home Cottage at midday waiting for his son Jamie to arrive. He hadn't seen him for a month or so, Jamie getting on with his life at the age of twenty-five, working at Argos in Camden Town. He was his only child thank God, a rough childhood thanks to Glenn's life of crime and then the split with Jamie's mother. Glenda now lived with another man up in Geordie land. Glenn hadn't seen her for years and Jamie only saw her every few years, if that. Glenn and Glenda. Almost the same name and just about the only thing they'd had in common in a marriage doomed to fail from the start. Just like thousands of others. At least she'd taken care of Jamie though until he was sixteen. Glenn was thankful of that. Then Jamie had left home and struck out on his own.

At ten past the hour he saw his son walking into the pub and waved him over to his table. They shook hands and Glenn went to the bar to buy him a pint. There were already twenty or so people in the pub; regulars who couldn't wait to start pouring alcohol down their throats.

When they were sitting down Glenn asked Jamie how things were going.

'Same old, same old,' Jamie said. 'How about you?'

'Definitely not the same old, same old.' Glenn said. 'I've got myself a new woman and I'd like you to meet her.'

Jamie almost choked on his first sip of John Smith's. 'A new woman? Where did you find her? Down the Job Centre?'

'Well, I didn't have to go looking far. She lives in my house on the first floor.'

Jamie smiled with disbelief. 'What, Hazy Daisy?'

Glenn smiled too. 'Yeah Hazy Daisy.' Glenn had told Jamie about Daisy's addiction problems before, and Jamie had come up with the nickname. He had never met her though.

'Jesus. I thought you said she was a nutter?'

'Well she is. Kind of. But now I'm starting to see the better side of her.' Like her butt, he almost added. He told him about their first two encounters and several more since. 'She seems quite keen on me. God knows why. I must be over twenty years older than her.'

'And you want me to meet her? She's coming to the pub? What about her husband?'

'She's not coming to the pub. She never goes out as far as I can tell. I'm going to take *you* to meet *her*.'

His son nodded. Glenn could see that Jamie didn't fancy the idea too much and who could blame him? Taking him back to his grotty lodgings to meet some flaky woman he'd never met before and had only heard bad things about.

'I don't know,' Jamie said. 'Do I really have to meet her? It might be over within a week. What's the point?'

'I'll tell you when we get there,' Glenn said. 'There's definitely a point. Now what would you like for lunch? This one's on me.'

They ordered a lasagne and chips each, and sat there talking about sport most of the time. Jamie also told him about his new friend Ray and some of the antics they were getting up to, like causing fights in bars, and stealing a guitar.

'Why do you need a guitar?' Glenn asked.

'Because I want to learn how to play,' Jamie reluctantly said.

'What's the point?'

'It's a good way to meet women.'

'How come?'

'Because they'll think I'm a shy sensitive kind instead of an arsehole.'

'Are you an arsehole?'

'To most women I am.'

Glenn nodded. He couldn't imagine his son playing a guitar. There wasn't a musical bone in his body. But there was no harm in trying, if that's what he wanted to waste his time on. And if it really helped him to get a woman… He would like to see his son get married someday, though he just couldn't imagine it somehow. Jamie walking down the aisle in a posh suit. No that definitely wouldn't happen. Maybe a registry office though, he could imagine that.

After two more pints Glenn was getting impatient to leave. He really wanted Jamie to meet Daisy.

They left the pub and walked down to the taxi rank at the station. The taxi driver wasn't too pleased to take them the short distance to Frenches Road. That was one of many reasons why Glenn would hate that particular job. Sit in the queue for hours then a punter like him comes along and asks for a cheap ride just a mile away. Then back to the queue for another few hours. What a way to make a living. Glenn glanced around for Scobie but couldn't see him anywhere.

Back at his lodgings, Glenn opened the front door and up they went to the first floor. They found Daisy in the living room watching a film on TV. Glenn glanced at the set and saw that it was James Bond, being played by Pierce Brosnan. Daisy looked up at the two of them and said hello to Jamie in a slurred voice. Glenn wondered which particular thing she was on today, pills or booze?

They left her there and went back down the few steps to the kitchen where Glenn put on the kettle.

Jamie said, 'She's not very talkative is she.'

'Not very,' Glenn said. 'But she puts out, that's the main thing.'

Jamie laughed. 'Puts out? I haven't heard that expression for a while.'

'I'm old fashioned,' Glenn said.

They sat at the small kitchen table and Glenn brought out a box of Mr Kipling cakes, white icing with a cherry on top.

Jamie took a bite of his and said, 'So where's the husband? Did he have to go to work or something?

You're walking around the kitchen almost as if you've moved in.'

Glenn looked at his son. He was no dummy. He knew something was up and he could smell a rat. 'Finish your tea and cake first and then I'll tell you.'

They ate with minimal conversation, the only sound being that of the TV, James Bond solving the world's problems by shooting and blowing things up. Glenn believed that most British men would trade anything to live the life of James Bond. Over the years he had become the country's most famous role model. Along with David Beckham. No wonder the country was going to hell.

When their tea was finished Glenn said, 'Let's go upstairs. There's something I have to show you.'

They went back past the living room, Daisy still sitting there engrossed.

Up on the top floor Glenn led Jamie straight into the bathroom. There was a blanket draped over the bath and he walked over to it and pulled it back. Vernon was lying there dead as a dodo.

Jamie took a step back in horror and pulled a face. 'Who the fuck is that?' he asked.

'That's Daisy's husband,' Glenn said. 'And I need you to help me get rid of him.'

Jamie pulled a face then stepped over to the toilet, got down on his hands and knees, and puked up his lasagne.

Glenn patted him on the back and pulled the flush when his son had finished.

'Don't worry,' he said. 'I've got a foolproof plan.'

Jamie looked up at him, red faced and ill looking. 'Jesus dad. I hope you know what you're doing.'

Glenn looked down at him and nodded. He had never felt so worried in his life, but with his son by his side he felt things would turn out okay.

## *CHAPTER TWELVE.*

They waited downstairs in the living room, watching the rest of James Bond and then some other crap that constituted Sunday evening TV. Jamie couldn't concentrate on any of it though. He kept thinking about the body upstairs in the bath.

He was sitting on the sofa next to his dad while Hazy Daisy sat to his right in an armchair, barely moving the whole time. She may as well be dead too, Jamie thought. How the hell had his father got mixed up with someone like that? Obviously the lure of some free sex had played a major part. He could see that her body wasn't too bad but her face was all red and bloated; he could make that out even in the dim light.

At seven p.m. he and his dad left the flat for some Chinese takeaway. Jamie was glad to be out of the place and into the fresh air. And he was feeling hungry, seeing as how he'd puked up all of his lunch.

'It all started,' his dad said as they walked along, 'when I came home from the pub one day and Daisy was by herself in the kitchen. She lifted up her dress and flashed me, and one thing led to another. Then she did the same the next day, except she came up to my room while Vernon was downstairs in the kitchen.'

'Blimey,' Jamie said. 'A bit risky.' He didn't really want to hear all the details, but it looked like he didn't have any choice in the matter. And his dad was talking to him as if he was his best mate, so maybe it wasn't so bad.

'Then, in the following week we did it three more times. Then yesterday I get a knock on my door, expecting to see Daisy once again, and it was Vernon. He says, "You must think I'm a fucking idiot or something. I know what's been going on from day one." Turns out that the first time Daisy and me had sex, when she wasn't wearing any underwear, she sat back down on the kitchen chair and, how shall I put it...'

Jamie looked at his dad, sure that some sordid details were about to come his way.

'She sat down on the chair and while she was there my spunk dribbled out of her and on to the chair.'

Jamie groaned.

'When she stood up to leave the room she left my mess in plain sight and Vernon saw it all there. Poor bloke had to clean it up.'

Jamie wondered if he might puke again. Then he found himself laughing. 'Jesus dad. That's the grossest thing I've ever heard.'

'Yeah well. Right away he got suspicious and kept his eye out. Then yesterday after telling me all that, he flipped and lunged at me. We grappled a while in my room...'

'Grappled? Your vocabulary dad is like twenty years out of date.'

'What's wrong with grappled?'

Jamie shook his head.

'We grappled in my room for about five minutes, most of it on the bed, me thinking, shit maybe Vernon wants to fuck me as well.'

Jamie laughed again.

'Then eventually I'd had enough. The only way to stop it was to kill the fucker. So I strangled him on the bed.'

Jamie was stunned and missed a step, making him almost stumble and fall. He knew his father was strong, but had never thought he might be capable of murder. But then again, if he was capable of armed robbery then why not murder? It was only a short step up. Or down.

'Then I dragged him into the bathroom and dumped him in the bath. I told Daisy that having a bath was vetoed for the moment. She was more upset about that than her husband. When I showed her the body she said, "He looks like a little boy with his mouth open."'

'Jesus,' Jamie said. 'She's all heart.'

His dad nodded. 'Yeah. Not the most sensitive of girls. She's got great nipples though. Very large areolas.'

Jamie wondered if he'd heard right. 'Orios? Like the biscuit? What the hell are those?'

'No not like the biscuit. Areola. The brown area around the nipple. Some women don't even have them. I like large areolas. Something about them.'

Jamie didn't have an opinion on the matter. Any tit was great as far as he was concerned.

They reached the Chinese takeaway and stepped inside. There was a small waiting area and a long partition behind which a small Chinese woman stood. They ordered an assortment of dishes plus rice and noodles, and sat down to wait. Jamie looked up at the TV screen high on the wall that was showing some awful quiz show, the sound turned down low. There were two other people waiting for their food.

Glenn looked up at the TV and said, 'Digital TV. I just don't see the attraction. And soon we'll all have to have digital radio too. It would be nice to have a choice in the matter.'

'I'm beginning to think that way too. We sell loads at Argos though. TVs and radios.'

'You enjoy it there do you? Any good looking members of staff?'

'Well most of them are black or Indian and I don't go for dark women. They're all friendly enough though.'

'From what I hear the white man will soon be in the minority in London.'

Jamie nodded. 'That's probably true already. Sometimes I feel like a stranger in a strange land.'

'Ever get a chance to steal anything?'

'No, it's all computerised. What would be the point anyway? It's all so cheap I may as well just buy something if I need it. And we get staff discount too.'

'That's good. Maybe I'll be buying some new stuff for our flat. Now that Vernon's out of the way.'

Jamie looked across at the other two people waiting, wondering if they could hear them. 'Well you can buy it in Redgate. They have an Argos.'

'I won't get your discount then though will I?'

'No, but at least you wouldn't have to come up to London.'

'I could order it through you to get the discount and then have it delivered.'

'Whatever. How will you be able to stay in the flat anyway? Won't someone miss Vernon? Like the people at his workplace?'

'Daisy's going to ring them tomorrow and tell them he's in hospital with something. It's only a small garage anyway. They won't give a shit.'

'And what about the flat? Won't the landlord notice something fishy?'

'Not at all. We just put the cash through his letter box every month. He never comes around. Me and Daisy can keep both flats going, no problem.'

'But how will you afford it? You can only just afford your own.'

'Well Daisy says they have some savings. That'll last a while until we figure out what to do. And maybe you can chip in at some time.'

Jamie felt his spirits nosedive even further. 'Great. All my hard earned cash going to a floozy called Daisy.'

'Careful what you say. She might be my future wife.'

Jamie could think of a dozen replies to that but bit his lip instead and sat in silence. Five minutes later their food arrived. He ended up paying for most of it, handing over a ten pound note while his dad chipped in with a fiver. It's already started, he thought; paying for the floozy Daisy.

They walked back up the road with the food in white plastic bags.

'What we're going to do,' his father said, 'is wait until after midnight, then take Vernon down to his car...'

'Vernon has a car?'

'Yes. Forgot to tell you that. A nice Polo. We can always sell that if we get short of money.'

'You've got it all planned.'

'We bundle Vernon into the car and take him up to the old Fuller's Earth quarry. We dump him over the side and let him rot down there. No one goes up there anymore. He'll never be found.'

'What, you don't want to bury him?'

'No, fuck that. Just let him rot away.'

'Okay. No digging is fine with me.'

'Who would want to be buried anyway? All those insects eating away at you.'

Jamie thought about that for a few seconds. 'But in the open air you'd get eaten by other things. What's the difference?'

His father shrugged. 'Yeah, but I'd prefer that. Or cremation.'

'I don't think we'll be cremating him,' Jamie said. 'But how the hell will I get to work tomorrow? I'm due in at ten.'

'Can't you ring up ill?'

'I don't really want to. Maybe I can take Vernon's car and drive home in that.'

'Yes you could do that. But what if you get stopped? That will blow the whole plan to smithereens straightaway. And you'll have to pay the congestion charge too.'

Jamie nodded. That was true. He didn't have a clue about how to pay the congestion charge. And he didn't want any *smithereens* either. Who the fuck thought up all these words in the first place? 'Maybe I'll just stay the night and leave really early. Catch the first train.'

'That would be better,' his dad said, as usual putting himself first and loading all the difficulties on to Jamie.

Back at the flat they dished up the food in the kitchen and ate it on their laps in the living room. Daisy still had the TV on, another film, something on Channel 5, they got all the crap movies. Jamie sat there with a full stomach, knowing he'd feel hungry again in an hour, and knowing that the time would pass really slowly until midnight.

He went to the kitchen and did the washing up, just to get away from this strange new woman, then sat on his own reading the Sunday paper with a cup of tea. His father came in now and then to see if he was okay.

'Yes I'm okay,' Jamie said, now in a bad mood. 'I just want to get it done and go home.'

His father left him alone until eleven-thirty, and then they went upstairs to sort out the body.

Actually there wasn't too much to do. Jamie's dad just wanted to dress Vernon in an old coat and hat and carry him out of the front door as if he was drunk. So that's what they did. Luckily Vernon had an old mac and also an old hat. They dressed him up as he lay there. Now he looked like a secret agent from an old black and white movie – except he was lying dead and stiff on the bathroom floor. He was beginning to smell a bit too. Jamie's dad said that Vernon had probably emptied his bowels. That just made Jamie feel sick again, wondering if his Chinese meal was about to make a quick exit as well. He managed to keep it down though, taking a few gasps of air through the open window.

Jamie couldn't believe he was actually doing this. It was a big leap from causing bar fights or feeling up the barmaid Gill's tits. Probably wasn't much of a stretch for his dad though, seeing as how he had such a varied criminal past. Jamie hadn't even seen a dead body before, not even in the street from a heart attack or car crash. It was all a very new experience.

When it was all done they lifted Vernon down the stairs to the first floor, Jamie taking the body, the heavy part, and then down the remaining stairs to the front hallway. There they left him leaning against the stairs, and went back up to see Daisy. She was still watching TV, hadn't even wanted one final look at Vernon. Something was wrong in her head, Jamie was sure. He wondered if she'd had a lobotomy at some time in her life. She was a puzzle with more than a few pieces missing.

Eventually the clock said half past midnight and Jamie's dad patted him on the knee and said, Let's do it. He kissed Daisy on the forehead as if he was going to work, and the two of them went down to the front hallway. Glenn picked up the car keys and walked down the street to the car, a bright red Polo, started it up and parked it right outside the front door.

He came back in and said, 'Well the street looks pretty clear. Shall we get it over with? We'll put him on the back seat, where all the drunkards go.'

Jamie nodded and they lifted Vernon up under his stiff arms and carried him out to the street. Glenn opened the Polo's back door, and they started shoving Vernon inside. Jamie had to go round to the other side to help the process along. After a few minutes Vernon was in, lying at an awkward angle, half on the seat and half on the floor. They climbed into the car and Glenn drove slowly away.

'Just pray we don't get stopped by the cops now,' he said. 'How would we explain this one away?'

'It doesn't bear thinking about,' Jamie said, then fell into a sulky silence.

They drove to Redgate town centre, past the station with a few taxis still waiting outside, then up the steep hill past the Home Cottage. Jamie looked at the quiet pub, thinking that just twelve hours ago he'd been sitting in there with his dad with no idea of the events that were about to unfold. He was now seriously thinking of cutting his dad out of his life for good. He didn't need his shit anymore, or even Vernon's shit, which was beginning to stink up the car. What kind of a father would get his son mixed up in such a thing?

At the top of the hill they followed the road out of town, and about a mile farther along they saw the skeleton of the old disused Fuller's Earth factory. Jamie knew that his dad had worked there once in his youth so he would know the layout of the place pretty well at least. He slowed the Polo and turned left off the main road and they trundled down an old tarmac track to the front gates. It was bolted with a very heavy looking chain but was at least out of sight of the main road.

'Now what?' Jamie said.

His father reversed the car and pulled it up sideways to the fence. 'Now we get Vernon out,' he said, 'lift him on to the roof and drop him over the fence. Then we climb over after him.'

So that's what they did.

Easier said than done.

At least it was fairly dark, not much chance of passing cars seeing them, though when they were standing on the Polo's roof their heads would have been visible to anyone looking from the road.

When all three of them were over the other side, two of them sweating and panting, Jamie said, 'What now?'

'Now we have to find some way of getting him to the quarry.'

'And how far is that?'

'About a ten minute walk. If you weren't carrying a body.'

Jamie shook his head in disbelief. 'Are you sure there aren't any security guards around here?'

'Positive. There's nothing worth stealing. I was talking to someone about it a few months ago.'

There's always something worth stealing, Jamie thought. Like lead or copper.

They left Vernon lying there and walked down the sloping drive, passing deserted buildings.

'That on the left,' said his dad, 'is the old locker room, and that is the canteen. That building on the right is the offices. Things were so simple in those days. One interview and you were in. A job for life.'

Jamie didn't really give a shit about the scenic tour. He just wanted to get the thing done. When they were past the old canteen he pointed to the left. 'Over there. A wheelbarrow.'

They walked over to where a pile of bricks and rubbish lay, on top of which was an old wheelbarrow. They hauled it off and it seemed to work okay. They wheeled it back up the road to where Vernon lay.

They lifted Vernon inside the barrow, put his hat on his chest, then Jamie took the handles and lifted. He was the fitter of the two so it would be a quicker walk if he carried the load. He trundled down the hill, his father nattering away about nothing by his side. After a few minutes they were into the factory proper and then had to find a route across the factory floor, most of the machines and fittings taken away, an empty shell of a building now. Jamie looked up at the roof, a tall building that would make a pretty nice abode if you were homeless. He wondered if any tramps were living there. Maybe one was watching them right now. He'd go to the police and ask for a reward for turning in a couple of murderers, then turn his life around with the loot received. Jamie almost smiled at the idea.

The dead weight of Vernon was not an easy one to push, despite the pretty good working order of the barrow. Jamie was sweating freely and stopped to take off his pullover. He draped it over a scrap of metal and said he'd pick it up on the way back. Then, when they reached the exit of the factory they came to problem number two.

The land on the quarry side was rutted and rough, scarred by tyre tracks, hard dirt that no one had walked over for years.

Jamie stopped the wheelbarrow and said, 'No way am I going to push him over this lot.'

'Let's carry him then,' his father said, heading for Vernon's feet of course, the lighter end of the load.

They lifted him out of the barrow and struggled with him across the land, tripping and losing their footing all the way to the quarry edge, a good five minutes of walking. They put the body down and Jamie stepped over to the edge and looked down, catching his breath. He knew for a fact that back in the old days they'd filmed some episodes of *Dr Who* here, down in the quarry, sci-fi monsters chasing the

Doctor through the clay valley. There were only two places in the UK where Fuller's Earth existed; Jamie couldn't remember where the other one was, maybe Southampton, or was it Bath? The earth was dug up, and after a succession of cleaning and drying processes was used for cosmetics and oil refining. Whenever Jamie had athletes foot, he knew that the powder he was sprinkling on his toes probably came from right here. Now that the factory had shut though – and he presumed the other UK one had closed too – he wondered just where the powder was coming from these days. Could be anywhere. Maybe that's why we invaded Iraq, he thought; turn all that desert sand into foot rot powder.

'Wake up sleepy head,' his father said next to him. 'Can you see a spot to drop him?'

Jamie shrugged. 'It all looks black to me. I guess here is as good a place as any.'

His father looked down. 'Yes that's a long drop. Just as well his coat's brown too. No one will see him at all.'

'Do you want to say some final words before we fling him?' Jamie asked.

His father looked down at Vernon's body. 'I never really knew him. What's to say?'

'Ashes to ashes, dust to dust?'

'Or kiss your arse goodbye Vernon.'

'I think he's already done that,' Jamie said.

They picked Vernon up, and after three swings, sent him out over the edge. They watched the body disappear into the dark and heard a faint thud as it landed somewhere down below. They peered over the edge into the dark.

'We are The Sultans of Swing,' Glenn said.

'He's in Dire Straits now,' Jamie said.

Glenn patted Jamie on the back. 'We'd make a good comedy team. Let's get back to Daisy. I'm bushed.'

'What about the wheelbarrow? Shall we send that over as well?'

'Might as well.'

So Jamie went back for the barrow and then swung that into the quarry too. There was a thud as it landed somewhere down below. Maybe it hit Vernon on the head Jamie thought. Or decapitated him.

They walked slowly and stiffly back the way they'd come. Jamie picked up his pullover en route and then they struggled over the fence which was pretty hard to climb without the car for help. That took a further twenty minutes and then they drove away.

Back at the house they climbed the stairs, two warriors returning from the exploits of the night. But Daisy was nowhere to be found.

'Maybe she's upstairs in the toilet,' Glenn said. 'You can have my bed. No way am I climbing another set of stairs.'

Jamie looked at his watch. It was one-thirty a.m. Five hours or so of sleep and then he'd have to get up to go back to London. He trudged up the final set of stairs and opened the bathroom door for a final wash and piss.

He stepped inside and lying in a steamy bath full of soap suds was Hazy Daisy. Jamie could see the tops of her breasts, and a bit of nipple too. She looked up at him with a lazy smile and winked.

Jamie had to agree with his dad; Daisy really did have large orios.

## CHAPTER THIRTEEN.

His mobile woke him up at six. At first he didn't know where he was, then remembered he was in his father's lumpy bed. He scrambled out from under the sheets which probably hadn't been washed for months, his body still stiff after last night's lifting. He took a wash at the sink and took a piss in there too. He didn't want to risk going in the bathroom just in case Daisy was there again. Crazy woman hadn't said a word last night – just smiled at him then looked down at his crutch - and Jamie had to leave pretty quickly and have a wash and piss in his dad's room, grateful that the old man had a sink in there.

He left the room and padded quietly down the stairs. There was no sign of life anywhere; no doubt his dad was flaked out in bed next to his new woman. Probably get an early morning blow job when he woke up as reward for getting rid of Vernon. Jamie carried on down the stairs and out of the front door.

He was relieved to be away, out in the fresh summer's air. If his dad had been awake he could have asked him for a lift to the station. Now he had to walk the twenty minutes or so but he didn't mind too much. Conversation with his dad would have been awkward. And he was still seriously thinking of cutting him off, getting him out of his life for good. Him and Hazy Daisy could form a life of their own now. If the body of Vernon wasn't found.

Jamie thought about the chances of that. Did anyone go for walks along the bottom of the quarry? Maybe *Dr Who* fans went down there to re-enact scenes from yesteryear. Maybe a lone jogger would come across the body; Vernon in his raincoat, his hat no longer on his head of course. He could be lying there in plain sight. Maybe he hadn't hit the bottom at all, was lying high up on a ledge somewhere, visible from the other side of the quarry. That was something to worry about. And what about wild animals? Maybe foxes would come along and eat him up. The bones would remain there for a long time and surely someone would find them eventually. Burying the body would have been a better idea. But too late for that now. And the ground would have been too hard to dig anyway.

In a corner shop he bought a Twix and a Marathon and a bottle of Coke and ate as he carried on walking, the sugar giving him a little boost of energy.

And what about the wheelbarrow? If that was found near the body then the cops would surely put two and two together. They would work out that Vernon had been wheeled there and dust the barrow for prints. And who had been the only one to touch the handles? Jamie tried to remember if his dad had touched them at all. He didn't think so. Maybe that had been intentional; let his son put his prints all over the barrow then leave it right next to the body as evidence. Christ, Jamie thought, now beginning to sweat. His dad had planted evidence against him! What kind of father would do that?

He reached the station ten minutes later having calmed down a little, but then had to buy another ticket which annoyed him even more. He trudged up the stairs to the platform and stood there waiting with early morning commuters: men in suits with briefcases looking like overgrown schoolboys, and nicely dressed office girls who didn't even glance at him. He wondered if he'd get a seat. Probably not. Dog tired and he'd have to stand like a dog all the way to Victoria. Then get on a tube or bus back to Camden. Go back to his flat, have a quick shower, change into some clean clothes, then a quick walk to work. Then bury his head in Argos objects and try and forget what had happened. What a strange Sunday it had turned out to be.

***

Jason Campbell spent most of Sunday round at Sara Shriver's house. It was his fourth visit there and now he'd been invited to meet her family - her film producer husband David, and her two teenage children Monty and Polly - plus several crew members from her last film.

There was a seventy-four year old director of photography called Nick, a blonde make-up girl in her late twenties called Candy, and a couple of European actresses, both dark haired and in their mid-thirties. Jason forgot their names as soon as he was introduced to them, walking in there, the last one to arrive, carrying an expensive bottle of Chablis that he hoped would be appreciated. He was then surprised to see that most of the bottles on the table were cheap ones that he recognised from various local supermarkets. So much for trying to impress the film star. Everyone was standing in the kitchen with their drinks, the food about to be served.

Jason felt a little uncomfortable as he was seated between one of the actresses, and the director of photography Nick. Jason listened to the conversation and smiled as he tucked into his dinner of chicken and ham, roast potatoes and vegetables. He couldn't remember the last time he'd had a Sunday roast; he certainly didn't bother with them living on his own. The meal had been made by Sara's husband David who fancied himself as a bit of a cook. Jason was impressed. It was the best meal he'd had for ages.

He learnt that Sara had returned from filming in Hungary just a week or so before Jason had met her on the tube. She'd been working on a quirky independent British film called *The Red Admiral* where she'd played the lesbian lover of the actress sitting right next to him. Her name was Chiara and she was in fact Italian. Jason asked when the film would be coming out and Sara said sometime next year. He was looking forward to seeing Sara and Chiara having sex on screen, but Sara said there was no nudity. Jason was a little disappointed. Then

Chiara said that she had filmed a masturbation scene seven times. Jason nearly choked on a roast potato. He was looking forward to seeing that scene as well.

The director of photography ate quietly next to him, only chipping in with comments when politics reared its ugly head as a topic of conversation. Jason listened quietly. He had always hated politics, had no interest in it at all. Going back to schooldays it was on a par with history as a subject he always avoided. Luckily one of his favourite Jackson Browne albums *For Everyman* was playing in the background so he listened to that instead.

When there was a lull in conversation Jason turned to Nick and said, 'So what are some of the famous films that you've worked on?'

Nick finished swallowing some food then said, 'Actually, my main claim to fame is that I filmed the John Lennon video 'Imagine'.'

The whole table fell silent in awe. 'You mean the one with the famous white piano?' Jason asked.

'Yes,' Nick said. 'I received a phone call from Yoko one day. She'd seen some of my other work, my short films. She said, "John's just written a new song and he'd like someone to film it." So I went round to their big house near Ascot and filmed it.'

'Blimey,' Jason said. 'That's impressive.'

'I also went around the world with John and Yoko while they did their peace in bed thing.'

'Jesus,' Jason said.

'In fact I was talking on the phone to Yoko a few weeks ago. She still rings me now and then. She

He fell silent again as Monty and Polly told some amusing stories about their schools. They were both in their mid teens, both at boarding school somewhere in Surrey. Jason wondered why parents gave their children such silly names. Was it all a joke to them? It was the children who had to live with them, though he had to admit that Monty and Polly both deserved their names. There was something slightly spoilt about them both.

As the meal was winding to an end, dessert finished – apple crumble, mustn't grumble – Rick said, 'Why don't you sing us all a song Jason? I'm sure the others would love to hear your whisky one.'

Jason groaned inwardly. Many times in his life he'd been asked to sing at parties and he generally disliked it. He felt like a performing monkey. And to top it off, he now had a man who'd filmed The Beatles and the Stones sitting right next to him. That would add an extra pressure.

'Are you going to play as well?' he asked Rick.

'Sure. I'll play a bit of lead.'

That made Jason feel better, and Rick left the room and came back with two guitars. He handed over his expensive Taylor to Jason and he put the capo on the second fret. 'Whisky Lingers' was always the song of his that people asked for, and Jason had never figured out just why. It was a good song all right but he had others that were just as good. Why this one in particular? It had four verses with the same chorus after each.

*'So fill my glass with two fingers, two fingers to you and the world, wine is fine but whisky lingers, and you will never be my girl.'*

He started picking away in the key of A minor and Rick joined in with some fancy lead work.

On the first chorus Sara joined in on backing vocals, sitting down the other end of the table next to Rick. The song sounded good, and four minutes later they finished to a rapturous round of applause from the others.

'Wow,' said David, Sara's husband. 'That's a great song. Maybe I can get it into a film for you.'

'That would be good,' Jason said. He didn't really know what else to say.

'We should film it and put it on You Tube,' Monty said. 'You should get a lot of hits.'

'That's a great idea,' Sara said. 'We'll do that another day. Maybe you could film it for us Nick?'

'Sure,' Nick said. 'I charge a hundred pounds an hour.'

The others laughed.

Sitting in such illustrious company was starting to make Jason's head spin. All things seemed possible at once. Maybe his music career was going to have a second wind after all, and maybe this second wind would blow all of his problems away.

They all retired to the music room later, with whiskies and brandies and other assorted drinks. Jason and Rick held forth, taking it in turns to entertain, Sara just joining in with the singing now and then. Even her daughter Polly played a few songs that she'd written, angst ridden teenager stuff with a Joni Mitchell influence. Or maybe it was Jessie J. Monty sat there with his iPhone and filmed a bit of it, Jason wondering which social network it would end up on. David the film producer got bored after a while and went to his office upstairs.

Back at home in the evening, his head still spinning from the adulation and the drink, Jason wondered if he was dreaming the whole thing. He was so glad he'd made the effort to talk to Sara when he'd seen her on the Underground that day. If he hadn't then none of this would have happened. Sometimes you just had to take a chance in life and see where things led.

He turned on the TV and started flicking through the channels, but TV seemed pretty boring right now. He had real life to take care of instead.

***

On Monday evening Jason was back at The Hope and Anchor, another two sets to be sung for the mighty total of £20. After Sunday's lunch he was wondering how long he would have to continue with these no hope gigs. Maybe David the film producer would really get 'Whisky Lingers' into a film and Jason would no longer have to work for a living. That big royalty cheque would come dropping through his letterbox one day and all of his problems would be solved. It was a nice dream to have.

He was looking forward to seeing Gill. He hadn't seen her for a while and had received no text messages either. But when he walked up to the bar and asked where she was a barman he'd never seen before said, 'Gill no longer works here. She left.'

Jason was stunned and disappointed. 'Yeah?' he said. 'When did she leave? And why?'

'Don't know,' said the new barman. 'I never met her. Ask Mike downstairs.'

Jason went down to the basement where Mike was setting up the equipment. Jason asked him where Gill had disappeared to.

'She was attacked a few weeks ago,' Mike said. 'Upstairs in the pool room.'

Jason couldn't believe what he was hearing and asked for more details. Mike told him.

'Shit,' Jason said. 'That's terrible. I wonder if she's okay. Maybe I should go and see her.'

'She's okay,' Mike said. 'She just doesn't want to work here anymore in case the two guys come back.'

'Did she report it to the police?'

'She did. But she didn't know their names. Just gave a description.'

Jason went to the bar stunned. He hadn't texted Gill for a while. He knew where she lived though, in a large shared house in Stoke Newington, so he could always go round sometime and see her. Coming to The Hope and Anchor wouldn't be much fun anymore though. She brightened up his evenings. Maybe he should pack this particular venue in as well. After all, the £20 made no difference to his life at all. He bought a bottle of Becks from another barman he'd never seen before, and sat on a stool.

The evening passed like many before it. Jason sang 'Whisky Lingers' in the first set and told the audience it might end up in a film. Just to get their attention. Most people just carried on talking though. Why should they give a shit? To them he was just another nobody. And an old one at that. With grey hair.

When his set was over he put his guitar behind the sound desk and went up to the street where he rang Gill on his mobile. When she picked up he asked how she was.

'I'm fine,' she said. 'Just a little paranoid about working in that place. I've got another job in another pub just around the corner from home. I don't know why I didn't do it before. It takes me five minutes to get to work instead of half an hour.'

'And who were these two guys who attacked you?' Jason asked. 'Had you seen them before?'

'Oh yes, I'd seen them before,' Gill said. 'They were those two that you were hanging out with.'

Jason didn't know who she was talking about. He hung out with so many people at The Hope. 'Which two guys?'

'Those two that started a fight one night when you were on stage. They came back a few weeks later and went up to the pool room. I think they were waiting for me to come up.'

'You mean Jamie and his weird friend Ray?'

'If that's what their names are.'

'Christ. I gave a guitar lesson to Jamie a week or so ago. He never mentioned a thing. I have his phone number. We can report him if you like. I knew there was something odd about him.'

'Let's do it,' Gill said. 'Can you give me his number and I'll pass it on to the police?'

'I'll text it to you in a minute.'

'Do you happen to know his surname?'

'I certainly do,' Jason said. 'It's Swell.'

'Jamie Swell? What a dumb name. How about the other idiot?'

'I don't know his surname. The police can find that out. That's what they're paid for.'

Jason hung up a few minutes later, then searched his mobile for Jamie's number and forwarded it. He felt a little guilty that he'd been the one to invite the two weirdo's down to the basement in the first place. But it wasn't his fault that they'd returned to do their dirty deed. Surely they'd been banned after that first fight anyway? Gill said she thought they'd been banned. He knew one thing for sure - he wouldn't be giving Jamie another guitar lesson. How could he bear being in the same room as the guy?

He went back down to the basement feeling a little better. At least Gill was okay and had another job and didn't seem to be mad with him. He waited for his second set to come around and chatted with a few new people. He found his mind wandering though and his spirits dipping a little. With Gill no longer in the bar how would he ever manage to see her again? He could ask her for a date over the phone or go to her new pub in Stoke Newington but it was such a difficult place to get to if you didn't have a car. He thought about these problems as the evening progressed.

When it was time for his second set, at twenty to eleven, he found himself going through the motions. He finished with 'I Fought the Law' but found the song repetitive and vowed never to sing it again. The crowd seemed to like it though, and he left the stage to a few half-hearted shouts of 'More!' Yeah, Jason thought. You'll be lucky. Maybe I'll never come back again. He said goodbye to Mike, picked up his £20, and headed for the street.

## CHAPTER FOURTEEN.

'I can't wait to see your lesbian scenes,' Rick said.

'They're nothing special,' Sara said. 'We kept our clothes on the whole time. We just had to do a bit of kissing and moaning.'

'I like watching women kiss,' Rick said. 'Something about it.'

'And when do you watch women kissing exactly?'

'On the Internet. Porn sites.'

Sara leaned on one arm and looked at Rick's naked body, the lower half covered by a sheet. 'I had no idea,' she said. 'And how often does this happen?'

'Not that often. Usually when I haven't seen you for a while.'

It was Monday afternoon, the day after the big Sunday lunch, Sara and Rick upstairs in the spare room. They'd been sleeping together for nearly a year now, unknown to Sara's husband David. Sara often wondered whether David would mind anyway. They hardly ever had sex, probably just a few times a year. He was more wrapped up in his production company than her, trying to get obscure films made in a British film industry that hardly existed anymore. Sara was the main breadwinner in the family, had been ever since they were married, and it was probably this fact that had made David lose his balls. He hardly had any sex drive these days and when he ejaculated hardly anything came out. Sara worried a little about that. Maybe David was ill. Maybe he had cancer or something. Or maybe, like Rick, he was watching too much porn.

'Here's a question for you,' Sara said. 'If a man masturbates a lot, does his sperm eventually run out?'

Rick chuckled. 'I have no idea. Why do you ask?'

'Because of David. And keep this to yourself. He just doesn't produce much anymore. I wonder if he masturbates too much.'

'What, in his office? Looking at porn during his lunch break? I doubt it.'

'You never know.'

Rick looked at her and said, 'Well it stands to reason that a man will not produce as much as he gets older. After all, David is in his mid-fifties. You can't keep shooting out bucket loads for your whole life.'

'I suppose not.'

'And the intensity will die as well. You'll end up with a floppy dick instead of a hard drive. I'm not looking forward to that day.'

'You have nothing to worry about in that department.'

'Not yet.'

'That's a good line - floppy dick and hard drive. Maybe you could write a comedy song about it. It might liven up our CD. Like Roger Miller used to do.'

'A bit before my time,' Rick said.

'Cheeky. He was a country legend.'

'Yeah. *England swings like a pendulum do.* I remember that one. Comedy songs might damage our artistic credibility. Not a bad idea for live shows though. For getting the audience on your side.'

'Do we have any artistic credibility?'

'That's a good question.'

Sara loved making love to Rick. He was twenty years younger than David and had a hard body from all his hours in the gym. His few years in the army had left him with the discipline to keep in shape and he could keep pounding her for an hour at a time no problem. Then he liked to come all over her breasts, tossing himself off while she tickled his balls. It was a sight to see. All that white stuff splashing all over her. She loved it. Poor David could only dream of producing so much.

Sara changed the subject. 'It was fun yesterday. Jason plays well. I think we're bringing out the best in him.'

'Yeah, he's a nice guy,' Rick said. 'A bit of a lonely guy too I think. Haven't heard him talk about a girlfriend or anything.'

'No. And he writes such good songs. I think we can use about three on the next album.'

'Yes, that'll give him a boost. Not that he'll make much money out of it.'

'Not with our sales.'

'Pretty pathetic really. I wonder if it'll ever take off.'

'Probably not. But that's not why we're doing it is it?'

'No, but a little success would be nice. And a few bigger concert venues would be nice too.' Rick scratched his shaved chest. Sara usually preferred hairy men, but a shaved chest was nice as well. It made him look even younger.

'I can't see it happening,' she said. 'If it was going to happen it would have happened after the first CD. But the reviews were pretty mediocre. Film stars singing is not something the music press particularly warm to.'

'No. You have to see it as a sideline really. Like Scarlett Johansson.'

'I like her CD. I wonder how many copies she sold.'

'Not many,' Rick said. 'I could probably find out.'

'Not that she needs to worry anyway. She must be making loads from films. More than I ever made, that's for sure.'

'Not getting bitter are we?' Rick said. 'Looking back at what might have been?'

'Maybe,' Sara said. 'Maybe that's why I'm sleeping with a younger man.'

'True.'

Ten minutes later they got out of bed and dressed. Then they went back down to the music room and worked on a couple of more songs. With three from Jason, they already had about ten for the next CD. Another couple would be enough. Rick liked short CDs, didn't like fourteen or fifteen songs, it was too many. A forty-five minute CD was all he aimed for, loves talking on the phone. I also did a few videos with Duran Duran and Ultravox. You've probably seen them. 'Rio' and 'Vienna'.'

'Of course,' Jason said. 'So you've worked in music more than film then?'

'Yes, that's fair to say. I also did some things with McCartney and George Harrison. Plus the Stones and Hendrix. Just look me up on IMDB, it'll give you a fairly accurate list.'

Jason said he would. 'Did you see the film *Nowhere Boy*?' he asked.

Nick nodded. 'A strange film. The actor playing John was far too good looking and had far too many muscles. John was a skinny lad when he was young, before they became The Beatles. The actor looked like he spent far too many hours in the gym. I don't think gyms even existed in the sixties. Except for boxers.'

'I thought that too,' Jason said. 'I thought you could tell that the director was in love with him. Too many lingering shots. And then they got married of course.'

'Yes,' Nick said. 'A strange one that.'

'They have different rules in film-land,' Jason said, and turned his head to see Sara looking right at him. Then she raised her eyebrows.

Nick nodded and went back to his eating.

Jason was in shock. Here he was sitting next to a man who'd worked with The Beatles, his favourite group of all time. He had all of their CDs – except *Yellow Submarine*.

and Sara had to agree with that. After all, back in the days of LPs, people just listened to one side and that was enough, probably twenty minutes or so. Then when CDs arrived people listened to the whole CD, anything from fifty to seventy minutes. It was too much, and did they even listen to the second half of the CD anyway? How had people changed their listening habits so drastically? And now with downloading it was going back to the other extreme, people just listening to single tracks by different artists all jumbled up on their latest electronic gadget. Sara despaired about the whole music industry. She hardly made a thing from streaming, such a pitiful amount of money for each track, especially on Spotify. Someone must be making some money somewhere, but she was pretty damned sure it wasn't the artists.

Rick played her a couple of songs that he'd found just last week, written by another local singer. They weren't as good as Jason's but still pretty good. Maybe they should just do a batch of local singers and call it *The Chiswick Album*.

At four o'clock Rick put down his Taylor and said he had to go home, he had a fitness lesson to take. She wondered where he got the energy from, especially after their love making. She watched him walk down the garden path then climb into his car, a shabby looking Citroen. She closed the front door and went upstairs for a shower. She had to wash the sex off before David came home, get her body back to its usual all-American girl look. Not too hard to do. Just like being an actress really. A different role for a different audience.

***

Rick Clayburn lived in a modern block of flats on the other side of Acton Park, just a two minute drive from Sara's house. When he'd first viewed the flat, the estate agent - a young blonde woman who he still saw occasionally driving around in a low pale green sports car with the estate agent's name written on the side and who he still fantasised about fucking - had said, "Ant and Dec used to live in this block. Before they were really famous." Like it was some kind of selling point. He didn't give a fuck about Ant and Dec but had bought the flat anyway, a modern one bedroom in a pretty soulless looking building.

Rick parked his Citroen in the car park round the back and went up to his flat, a quick walk up three flights of stairs. He never used the lift. He didn't trust them and the climb was good for his leg muscles and knees.

From his third floor window he could see the brightly coloured graffiti mosaic house about a hundred yards away, a building and street wall covered in political words and pictures which was never painted over for some reason, giving it the air of a relic from the 1960s. People often stopped to look at the artful creation, usually children with their parents. Maybe that was why it was never painted over – it kept the locals entertained while adding some much needed character to the area.

Rick had two more guitars in his living room apart from the Taylor that he left permanently at Sara's – a Levin and a Larrivee. Also a Yamaha keyboard sitting on a stand in the corner that he had never mastered. There was something about the piano that he could never really figure out. Maybe he just didn't have the brains for it or the coordination. The guitar was his instrument and that was fine with him. After all, he hardly had any pianists in his CD collection – only Elton John sprang to mind – so what was the point of learning it? Better just to stay as a guitar man, that's where he felt comfortable. His favourite guitarist was Nils Lofgren. He had a Lofgren DVD showing all his licks and tricks, a baffling array of acoustic and electric artistry. If he could get as good as Nils one day he would die a happy man.

Rick slumped down on to his settee and closed his eyes, thought about Sara and her naked body. He still couldn't believe that he had a film star as his lover. It was something he wanted to shout about to the rest of the world – or at least put on Facebook – but he couldn't for obvious reasons. He had met her a little over a year ago when she'd been putting her band together and was looking for musicians. He'd been recommended to her by an actor friend and they'd hit it off straightaway and had ended up in bed after only a month. Rick had been amazed at the time, but after reading a few film books like *Easy*

*Riders, Raging Bulls,* he reckoned that most of the film world, and especially actors, ended up in bed together before you could say *And the Oscar goes to.* It had made him slightly envious, all these beautiful people fucking each other, but at least he now had one of them for himself. He guessed it would all fizzle out eventually and end in tears, but it was good for now and the music was fun too.

Rick had played in various bands over the years, never progressing much higher than the pub circuit, but now that he was with Sara they were playing minor concert halls and such, and he felt he was moving up. Not that he had too much to move up to. At thirty-five he was too old to make much of an impact in the music industry, but if he could get some of his songs out there he could make some extra pocket money. Just like Jason was hoping to do. It only took one big artist to notice one of your songs, record it themselves, and some good money would start rolling in. Like that unknown guy who'd written *Angels* for Robbie Williams and was now a multi-millionaire, when most punters thought that Williams had actually written the song. It was now the most popular song played at funerals too, overtaking the theme tune to *Match of the Day.*

Rick was barely scraping by at the moment, though he gave off the air of someone who was quite successful. He had five part-time jobs, none of them really raking in the cash: he was a part-time barman at the The Duke of Sussex pub down the road, he did a little web design for various friends and acquaintances, he was a musician and bit-part actor, and he was also a personal trainer. Sometimes he felt he was also a magician, juggling all those jobs at once and keeping everything ticking over, just to pay the mortgage and the bills.

He looked at his watch. At six o'clock he had a fitness lesson. It was a good way of meeting loose women, usually bored housewives who enjoyed being taken to a park and being put through some moves by a muscle-bound youngish man. And if he was lucky, some of them invited him back to their house for a quick shag before their husband came home.

When he'd first started as a trainer, back in his late-twenties, he was averaging five new women every year; he'd kept a note of them all in his training log. Some of them were young and single, wanting a slightly older man who'd been around the block a few times, but most of them were older. They were easier to get into bed than younger women, the only drawback being the state of some of their bodies, but once he was up and running he seemed to forget about all that quite quickly. But since he'd met Sara, Rick had cut out all the extra activity, thinking he didn't want to blow a good thing now that he was with a film star. And who could match up to Sara anyway? She was a fine looking woman and still had a great body. None of his fitness clients could match up to her in any way. And he found most of them boring now too. Sara had so many good stories to tell – about all the films she'd worked on, all the famous actors she'd bedded – that all the rest just seemed insignificant.

He walked into the bathroom, stripped off and stepped into the shower. Maybe he could write a song called 'Personal Trainer'. *I'm your personal trainer baby, gonna make some exercise with you. Get your body into shape, then do all the things I wanna do.* It had possibilities.

After towelling off and dressing in a tracksuit, he left the flat and went back down to his car. Though the park was only a few minutes walk away, he preferred taking the Citroen as all of his training gear was in the boot: weights, mats, bottles of water and energy drink, boxing gloves (some women liked to punch the shit out of his open hands while no doubt wishing it was their husband's head), heat rub, Vaseline, even condoms. He never knew what might come in handy.

Parking by the side of the park he saw his latest new pupil Mandy already there, sitting on a bench. She had a nice figure and a great cleavage, and back in the old days he would have pursued her but not now. He climbed out of the Citroen and wandered over; Mr Faithful, keeping his thoughts and his hands to himself.

It was a warm evening and an hour of gentle sweating on the grass was a good way to end the day. Then he could go home, cook a healthy meal, and pick away on guitar. A pretty good life really – if only he was making a bit more money.

## CHAPTER FIFTEEN.

On Tuesday evening after a busy day at Argos, Jamie Swell received a knock on the front door of his council flat. He opened it to find two police people standing there, a man in plainclothes and a woman in uniform. Jamie's first thought was Shit, they've found Vernon's body already! But after asking them what it was all about he was relieved to find that it was only about the assault on the barmaid in Islington – apparently Gill Anderson was her full name. For some reason the name sounded familiar.

They all sat down in the living room and the policeman said, 'We've received a complaint about you attacking and molesting a barmaid at The Hope and Anchor pub in Islington, on the night of ....' He looked down at his notebook for clarification.

Jamie nodded. What was the point in denying it? 'I didn't start it though,' he said weakly. 'It was my friend Ray. You probably know that by now anyway.' Why should he protect Ray when he'd been the one getting them into trouble recently?

The two police people looked at each other and the man said, 'And what's Ray's surname?'

Jamie swore to himself. So they didn't know about Ray at all. So who the hell had told them that *he* was involved? He couldn't think of anyone.

'Lane,' he said meekly. 'Ray Lane.'

'And where does this Ray Lane live?'

'Somewhere in Essex,' Jamie said. 'I'm not sure of the town. I've never been to his place. I don't know him that well really.'

'Can you give us his phone number?' the policeman asked.

Jamie picked up his mobile from the coffee table, found Ray's number and read it out.

'Thanks,' said the policeman. 'That'll be enough to find him. That's how we found you.'

'Yeah?' Jamie said. 'Who gave you my number then? I don't have that many friends.'

'I'm not at liberty to say,' the policeman said. 'Someone came forward.'

Jamie was puzzled. He would check all the numbers on his phone when they were gone and work out who it was. He looked over at the policewoman, who hadn't said a word yet, and smiled. She didn't smile back.

'You'll have to come down to the station and make a statement,' the policeman said. 'Right now if that's okay.'

Jamie shrugged. 'Fine with me. There's nothing on TV.'

And the three of them left the flat.

\*\*\*

Back at home after ten o'clock – released on bail, with a court appearance pending - Jamie sat on the sofa and flicked through his mobile contacts. He only had about twenty people on there, and six of those were work colleagues. It only took a few minutes to figure out who it was; it must be Jason Campbell the guitar teacher.

Jason was tight with Gill, so obviously had her phone number. Gill must have told him about the attack, then Jason told her that he had Jamie's number; all because Jamie had wanted a guitar lesson, something that he'd lost interest in already. He glanced across the room at the crimson guitar leaning against the wall. If it wasn't for the guitar and then taking a lesson he would have got away with it. One guitar causing him so much trouble. Maybe he was getting payback for stealing it in the first place. Since his lesson with Jason it had got itself all out of tune and he hadn't bothered re-tuning it. What was the point? He would never master it anyway.

He wondered whether he should ring Ray and tell him that the police were on their way. He decided not to. Fuck him. He could get a nasty surprise, just the way Jamie had done. This would probably be the end of their friendship but that was no big loss. He was getting sick of people getting him into trouble. First Ray and now his dad as well. He wondered how long it would take for Vernon's body to be found. Maybe he would be in jail by the end of the year. Christmas in prison. What a thought.

The police had told him that once they'd questioned Ray the two of them would be given a date in court. Jamie wasn't that worried really. As he had no priors he was pretty sure he'd get away with a fine or a suspended sentence. After all, he hadn't really done that much, just watched as Ray did all of the attacking and then most of the molesting.

He thought back to the fateful night. He remembered getting a feel of Gill's tits but he hadn't done much else. Maybe held her down as well, he really couldn't remember. It reminded him a little of that old Jodie Foster film where she'd been raped in a bar by several men in front of a baying crowd. At the first trial the men hadn't even been prosecuted, but had been prosecuted at the second trial for something else, he couldn't really remember what it was. So if they'd got away with it, surely he and Ray would too, as they hadn't even raped her. It was all a big fuss about nothing as far as he was concerned. His main worry was still the body of Vernon, down in the Fuller's Earth quarry.

He fetched a can of beer from the fridge and turned on the TV, then flicked through the channels without being able to concentrate.

***

'How are you feeling about things?' Glenn said. 'You don't talk much.'

Daisy lay next to him in the double bed and didn't even look at him, just kept staring at the ceiling. It was Wednesday morning, the curtains slightly drawn, Glenn taking over Vernon's vacated place in the master bedroom. He'd slept there three nights in a row, ever since dumping Vernon's body into the

Fuller's Earth quarry. Glenn had dreamt about the incident several times since – dreams like horror films, talking to Vernon as he arose from a swamp all covered in mud - but it didn't worry him too much. He wasn't a believer in dreams and their significance, thought they were just a load of baloney, the mind playing tricks as it revived itself. He wondered what state Vernon's body would be in by now though and if it was well hidden. Maybe he should go over to the quarry some time and have a look.

'Fine,' Daisy said.

'What about Vernon?' Glenn asked. 'Do you miss him?'

'No,' Daisy said, still looking at the ceiling.

They were having sex once or twice a day, like young lovers who couldn't get enough of each other. But Daisy didn't respond to his attempts at conversation; he wondered if she even knew what it was. She hadn't asked him any questions about himself and his interesting life and that was a subject he loved talking about. He needed conversation. He had spent too many years on his own, either in prison cells or cheap lodgings, and liked to talk when the occasion arose. He didn't really want to hang around with a silent woman even if she was fulfilling his sexual needs.

Maybe when he got bored with all the physicality he would just move out, but that would present a whole new set of problems. How would Daisy respond if he disappeared? And how would he be able to find another place to live when he was an out of work ex-con? Plus he still had to sign on with the Job Centre and the Work Programme so he couldn't move too far away.

Also, Daisy probably couldn't cope with living on her own and she was bound to blab to someone eventually about her poor husband's death. That would mean another trip back to jail, probably for fifteen years this time. He couldn't handle that. He'd rather hang himself in his cell.

He climbed out of bed and drew the curtains. The view outside was the brick wall of the house next door. A lady in her fifties lived there alone, a nice woman with dyed red hair who he'd chatted to a few times. Maybe he should move in with her instead, at least there'd be some conversation. She was fairly attractive too, short, with a nice curvy figure.

He went to the kitchen in his boxer shorts and made some tea and toast. Daisy appeared eventually and sat down at the table in silence. Her eyes looked spaced out.

'Want to go for a walk later?' he asked.

Daisy shook her head. 'Too risky. Can't be seen together.'

Glenn nodded. He had to agree with that, what was he thinking? 'I'm going to go for a walk. Let me know what food we need and I'll get it on the way back.'

Daisy nodded. Her face was always bright red in the morning, as if the pills she was taking worked overtime at night. He had found her stash in a kitchen drawer yesterday and looked at the labels, but the names didn't mean anything to him, he couldn't even read half of them. He reckoned she was taking about ten pills a day. Surely she couldn't keep that up for life. She would surely burn herself out - or explode.

An hour later, after a shit and a shower, Glenn left the house with a shopping list, crossed the road, and walked over to the Holmethorpe Industrial Estate. He passed under the railway bridge at the entrance and headed straight down the rutted track that led to the old British Industrial Sand factory. Like Fuller's Earth, BIS had also closed down many years ago, leaving a metal skeleton against the skyline. It took Glenn ten minutes to reach it, walking across barren land which he'd heard would soon be redeveloped; small warehouses and blocks of flats were going to be built there. Then he headed left towards what used to be a builder's merchants yard. That had also closed down many years ago, following the murder of the elderly gentleman who used to run it. He'd been pushed over the edge into the quarry by a psycho on a murder spree. Glenn remembered the psycho's name as Phil Gator; it had been all over the papers and TV at the time. Glenn had been in prison when it happened. He had felt almost proud that the town of Redgate was once again making the news, so many years after the Great Train robber Ronnie Biggs. It had been something to brag about to the other prisoners, his connection to the town, and also to Mr Biggs.

Glenn spotted a few men as he walked, all of them wearing yellow hard hats. He wondered if someone would stop him for not wearing one. Five minutes later he came to the old builder's merchants and walked through the yard, a few stacks of old pipes and fittings still lying around, but mostly smashed or cracked by vandals. Then he came to the far side of the yard, the place where the old man had fallen to his death. The ground fell away in a sandy slope, more broken pipes and fittings down at the bottom. Glenn looked over the quarry to the other side, the Fuller's Earth side, and looked up to the top, trying to figure out just where he and Jamie had dumped Vernon over, but it was impossible to tell.

He walked along the sandy bank for a few minutes still glancing over, but the bottom of the quarry was overgrown with small trees and shrubs and there was no way he would be able to spot a body, or even a wheelbarrow from where he was. To do that, he would have to slide down the sandy bank and into the quarry, and then walk along amongst all the greenery. He didn't really want to do that. There was no telling what was down there. Maybe he'd fall into some quicksand or something or get attacked by foxes. Or maybe there were snakes. It wasn't worth the risk. And what if someone came along and saw him? They might stop him for a chat, ask him what he was looking for. No, he was satisfied with what he'd found. If Vernon's body had fallen all the way to the bottom then it would be safely covered by shrubs for quite a while. And because the place was so overgrown, surely no one would walk along there for a Sunday morning stroll. Or any other day of the week for that matter.

Feeling better than he had an hour ago, Glenn left the area and headed back offsite. Now he would have to go and do some food shopping. Maybe he could take Vernon's car and go to a proper supermarket for a change. That would be a treat. Buy Daisy some healthy food instead of all the frozen crap she ate. Maybe it would loosen her brain a little and they could have a decent conversation for once.

As he was crossing the road in front of his house, he saw the red headed woman from next door just about to climb into her little Ford Fiesta. Glenn waved at her and jogged across the road. She waited by the car for him and said hello.

'Where are you off to then?' he asked.

'Morrisons,' the woman said. 'For my weekly shop.' She smiled at him in a nice way and Glenn felt encouraged to be a bit cheeky.

'Any chance I could come with you?' he asked. 'I need to get some food too.'

The woman smiled again and said, 'Of course. Jump in.'

Glenn walked around to the other side of the car and waited for her to unlock the door. As they were driving along he noticed a magnet on the dashboard that said simply *Angie*. Of course. He remembered now that her name was Angela. She had told him once. He wondered if she remembered his name. He doubted it. Then he remembered the old Rolling Stones song called 'Angie'. He sang a few words out loud and she looked at him and laughed. He knew they would get along just fine.

## *CHAPTER SIXTEEN.*

After his final teaching lesson of the day at five o'clock, Jason left his flat and made the short walk to South Acton Overground station. He'd arranged to meet Gill later, so he had to make the awkward journey to Stoke Newington in North London which would take him over an hour. As he was waiting for his train, standing on the platform with commuters and a few schoolchildren, he felt the mobile in his pocket buzz with an incoming text. He took it out hoping that it wasn't Gill cancelling and saw that it was from Jamie Swell. It read:

*Thanx for dumping me in the shit tosser. U no wot happens 2 grasses don't u? Ud better watch your back gitar man.*

Jason was shocked by the threat. He looked up and down the platform, half expecting to see Jamie loitering somewhere. He wondered if he should text him back but what was the point? Did Jamie really expect him to keep quiet when he'd assaulted his favourite woman in the world? The guy was clearly deranged. He wondered what the police had said to him and if he'd been charged yet. Maybe Gill would know.

The train arrived and Jason found a seat. It was fairly empty but would be heaving by the time it reached Dalston Kingsland which was more than ten stops away. He took a book from his bag, a biography of Tom Waits, and tried reading, but the annoying text message kept popping into his head and he couldn't concentrate. Any threat to his wellbeing automatically brought back thoughts of his previous life in Woodvale. He didn't want to go through a similar situation again, didn't want to be hiding out or looking over his shoulder all the time for Jamie or Ray to appear. It would be like the Teddy Peppers situation all over again. *Just like Teddy*. What a drag that would be. Jason started singing to himself the old Heinz song called 'Just Like Eddie'. It lifted his mood a little.

Or maybe he was more to blame than he thought. Maybe he brought all these situations on himself by trusting and befriending people he shouldn't. Maybe it was a case of *Just Like Jason*, the same mistakes being made over and over. His mood went down a little again.

About forty minutes later he arrived at his station and went up the stairs to the street. He'd managed to read just five pages of his book. Not as much as he'd hoped for.

When the appropriate bus arrived, he stood all the way as it crawled along in the rush hour traffic. Fifteen minutes later he reached his stop and was thankful to get out into the fresh air. He crossed the road and started walking towards Gill's house.

He had been there just once before, her birthday party last year. The invite had said to come in fancy dress as a 'music icon', so Jason had simply gone as himself, he couldn't think of anyone else. Not many of the others had made an effort either. There had been one guy dressed as Elvis, a good looking lesbian dressed as David Bowie, another girl dressed as Beethoven, plus the usual mix of punks and Goths. Jason had spent the entire evening feeling uncomfortable as most of the people there were twenty years younger than him. That was the problem of still being single in his fifties: all of his old friends were married so they rarely invited him over, while his other friends tended to be a lot younger. Which was fine for meeting up in a pub or café, but at a party could be a bit excluding.

As Jason made the ten minute walk to Gill's house he passed quite a few Jewish people strolling along, some of them wearing massive black furry hats, others with long curly dark hair. In a way he envied them their beliefs and the strict way their lives must be structured. He had no structure or beliefs in his own life, just the simple objective of having to make enough money to survive. It wasn't much of a way to carry on. And now he had the extra worry of someone maybe looking to beat him up. It was this thought that was in his head when he rang Gill's front doorbell.

There was a loud barking from inside and a dog rushed up to the door. Jason remembered that Gill, in the house she shared with about five others, owned a large friendly Alsatian called Santini. Friendly until someone rang the front doorbell that is.

Gill opened the door and let him in, holding Santini back by the collar. Gill was wearing jeans and a pink T-shirt, her large breasts moving around as usual. Jason tried not to look but managed a quick peak. He kissed her on the cheek, patted Santini on the head, and she led him along the corridor and down a few steps into the kitchen. Laid out on the table were a few salad bowls and plates for supper, plus a bottle of white wine and large glasses. Jason handed her another bottle of white that he'd brought. Gill put some more bowls on the table - she was a vegetarian - and poured out the wine. Jason started spooning assorted beans and greens on to his plate.

He told her straightaway about the text he'd just received from Jamie and she told him in detail about the attack in the pub. Jason was astounded that the two of them would try something so audacious, such a random attack that could have grievous consequences for them both. Now that Jamie had been caught it would affect the rest of his life, a criminal record that would follow him no matter where he worked. Was it worth it just for a sighting and feel of Gill's breasts? Jason had to admit that it might well be worth it.

'I'll tell my friendly policeman about the text,' Gill said. 'Don't delete it. It might come in useful later.'

'I won't,' Jason said. 'In fact it's stone cold evidence that he's admitting that he did it. He's a fool if he thinks he's going to get away with it.'

'I'll make a note of the exact words before you leave. Now that I'm also an investigative journalist these days.'

Jason wondered if he'd heard correctly. 'What was that?'

'I've just been commissioned to write an article for the Sunday Times magazine.'

'Great,' Jason said. 'I didn't know you were a writer as well.'

'I do a bit. I just don't tell anyone.'

'So, tell me more.'

Gill took a sip of wine. 'When I was on holiday last year in California I met a guy in a bar who turned out to be a bounty hunter. As I was talking to him I thought he'd be a great subject for an article. I asked if he'd mind being written about, and being American, he jumped at the chance. They're always after some self promotion.'

'So you interviewed him while you were there?'

'Yes. I bought a voice recorder and met with him several times. When I came home I started writing and now I have enough for an article. We also email about once a week.'

'Amazing. Well done. Maybe it'll lead to other writing jobs as well.'

'That's what I'm hoping for. I don't want to be working in bars my whole life. Especially after what's just happened.'

'Maybe this guy could come over here, and sort out Jamie and Ray.'

'Maybe he could. He does do a bit of travelling as well.'

'What's his name?'

'Lance Boyle. Though I don't think that's his real name. He has a shady past which he won't tell me about.'

'Lance Boyle? You're kidding,' Jason said with a smile. 'Does his middle name begin with an A?'

'What's so funny?'

'Lance a boil, that's what's funny.'

'Whatever amuses you. Maybe that's why he chose that name. I told you I didn't think it was real.'

'He sounds like a good character for a film. Maybe you could write a screenplay next.'

Gill nodded. 'I emailed him about what just happened and he really did want to fly over. I think he fancies me.'

'I can't imagine why,' Jason said.

He felt slightly jealous, and wondered if Gill was about to disappear from the country for good and wind up living in California with a bounty hunter. What were his chances of ending up with her when he was up against such a macho man?

Gill smiled. 'Don't worry,' she said. 'You're still my favourite guitar man.'

Jason felt himself blushing and shoved some bean salad into his mouth.

***

When the meal was over they went into the living room where an old dobro lay on the sofa. Jason picked it up and played 'Hey Gill'. Though Gill had heard it before in The Hope she hadn't really been listening to the lyrics as she'd been serving people. She found it highly amusing this time round, though Jason thought the song was fairly serious. Santini lay on the floor half asleep, looking at him, clearly unimpressed.

Jason played another song he'd written recently and then a couple of Gill's housemates turned up, people even younger than Gill who he'd met before. Jason put the dobro down and had a quick chat with them. Then Gill said she'd show him her new place of work.

They left the house and headed back towards the main road. Her new pub was called The Crow's Nest; it was fairly large with a rectangular bar in the centre. There was a very attractive young lady with long dark hair working behind the bar called Mary Ann. Gill introduced her to Jason. She was probably only thirty, and once again Jason felt like an old man. She was wearing a short black skirt and stunning fishnet tights. When she walked away from him Jason couldn't take his eyes off her.

'Quite a beauty isn't she?' Gill said.

'Yes,' Jason managed to force out, feeling a little hoarse.

They took their drinks to a table and sat down.

The bar started to fill up and at nine o'clock an open mic started. Gill hadn't told him there was an open mic until they'd arrived, and Jason was quite pleased to watch a bit of music. Gill went up to the guy running the show and put Jason's name on the list. He hadn't wanted to sing, but now that he'd met Mary Ann, he was quite keen to show off in front of her. When his name came up he borrowed someone's guitar and stepped on to the low stage.

There were about fifty people in the pub now and the first song he did was one called 'Life is a Road', a song he had written quite a few years ago and which always went down well. He received a good round of applause afterwards, and then he sang the song that Sara Shriver was impressed with, 'Whisky Lingers'. Not one to waste an opportunity, he dedicated the song to Mary Ann who looked over at him with surprise at the mention of her name. She smiled at him and Jason sang the song with extra feeling, receiving another good round of applause. Then he left the stage and went back to sit with Gill.

'That was a nice touch,' she said. 'Dedicating a song to Mary Ann. Why don't you ask for her number?'

Jason shook his head. 'She's far too young.'

'She's thirty-two,' Gill said. 'And single. That means she's within the twenty year gap range, on the cusp of respectability.'

Jason nodded and looked over at the bar. He'd had a few affairs with women who were twenty years younger than him, but never a relationship. He thought the age difference was just too wide. A shame it wasn't fifteen years. He felt that age gap could work in a relationship.

'Maybe you can just give me her number and then I can think about it?' he said.

'I could do that,' Gill said. 'Coward.'

Jason couldn't disagree. He *was* a coward. Both in relationships and in real life.

When they left the bar an hour later he was still feeling paranoid about being attacked, keeping an eye on the people walking up to him, then standing with his back against a building while waiting for a bus. He felt inadequate, like a weakling. He was willing to bet this Lance Boyle didn't feel like a coward when walking down the street. Especially now that it seemed he was moving in on Gill. What a bummer that was.

A bus came along a few minutes later, and as Jason climbed on board he was cheered by the fact that he had Mary Ann's phone number in his pocket. One bus moves away and another comes along to take its place. Maybe there was a song in there somewhere.

## CHAPTER SEVENTEEN.

Things were getting complicated.

Glenn woke up early on Thursday morning and lay in bed looking at the drawn curtains on the bedroom window. If he stared at them long enough maybe he could see right through them, then through the brick wall of the house next door and into the bedroom where Angie lay - the new focus of his attention.

They'd had a fun time together down at Redgate Morrisons yesterday, both of them with trolleys, wheeling them around, gathering their bits of food. Angie was amazed at the amount that Glenn was buying and he had to lie to her by saying that he had a large fridge-freezer in his room. He couldn't tell her that he was buying food for two, using a wad of cash that Daisy had given him. They'd compared prices on things and talked about their food likes and dislikes. Glenn had never imagined that being in a supermarket could be so enjoyable.

Angie was easy to joke with and had a nice pleasant laugh. Had he ever heard Daisy laugh? He didn't think so. Glenn had been bowled over by Angie he had to admit. Why had he never noticed all this about her before? Well, the answer to that was simple. He had never spent any length of time with her before, had only had the briefest of chats as they passed each other outside, usually when she was pottering around in her garden. He'd also never had the confidence to talk to her before, thinking that she must know everything about him, his criminal past and such, and wouldn't want to touch him with a bargepole. But in a strange way, his fling with Daisy had given him some much needed confidence, made him feel that maybe some women found him attractive after all.

In a rough kind of way he was a pretty good looking chap, but in recent years he'd begun to get a complex about his grey hair and the extra wrinkles on his face and the bags beneath his eyes. When he looked in the mirror he just didn't recognise the face looking back at him anymore. He still had the mind of a twenty year old so why did he have the face of a fifty-eight year old? It just didn't make sense.

But the way Daisy had seduced him had given him a lift, even though she wasn't the brightest spark in the playground. Daisy was only thirty-five and still had a good figure, and if someone of that age wanted to seduce him then maybe things weren't as bad as he'd imagined. So he'd felt good being with Angie, had laughed and joked with confidence, and when they'd returned home she'd invited him inside for a cup of tea.

'I have to get my food indoors,' Glenn had offered as a weak excuse. He'd already left Daisy alone for a few hours. How on earth could he disappear next door for tea?

But when he'd taken the food up to the flat, put it all in the fridge-freezer, he'd found Daisy sitting in the living room, once again with the TV on. She'd hardly looked at him when he walked in.

'How's it going?' he'd asked her.

'Okay,' she'd said.

Glenn had thought, to hell with her. 'I'm going to pop out again.'

'Fine,' she'd said, without moving her eyes towards him.

So Glenn had gone back downstairs and round to Angie's, rung the front doorbell, and told her he'd changed his mind.

She'd sat him in her small living room - old style furniture and terrible paintings on the walls, like the kind you'd pick up for nothing at a jumble sale – and disappeared to the kitchen to make some tea. Five minutes later she'd reappeared with a tray, cups and saucers and a tin of biscuits. Then she'd played mother, pouring everything out, and Glenn couldn't remember the last time he'd drunk tea out of a cup with a saucer. In his large hands the cup looked like something out of a child's doll's house.

After talking about nothing much for twenty minutes or so, Angie had then got out her old photo album and sat right next to him on the sofa showing him her whole life story in a series of black and white, and then colour photos. Glenn had found her voice incredibly soothing, had felt his head swimming in a nice relaxed way. He'd wanted to just fall asleep on her lap as she stroked his head, the way his mother had done when he was a boy. He'd almost had to pinch himself to stop his eyes from closing, the power of her voice had been so great. Imagine what that voice would be like in bed, he'd thought. That soothing sound as he was entering her. It was an image he couldn't get rid of, and he found his prick rising as he thought about her now.

And he'd risen to the occasion while he was looking at her photo album too. The album had been resting on his lap and Angie was leaning over him and pointing down at the photos and pressing the book now and then. If you took away the book her hand was only about an inch away from his cock. He'd felt himself getting hard and then his erection had started nudging the album, making it rise and fall in little surges. Glenn was pretty sure that Angie hadn't noticed though. She was somehow too innocent to notice such things. When she'd come to the end of the photo session she'd reached right across him to take the album away and her ginger hair was only inches from his face. He could smell her shampoo. Then she'd taken the album, stood up, and put it back on the bookshelf she'd taken it from.

Back in her own armchair, they'd talked some more, Glenn relaxing again as his hard on disappeared. Angie had been married once but her husband had died from cancer when he was in his forties. She had a son aged eighteen who'd left home a year ago and was now living in Horley and working at Gatwick Airport as a cleaner. He visited her most weekends. Glenn told her about Jamie and how he worked for Argos.

'Are you close?' Angie had asked.

'Sometimes,' Glenn had replied. When we're dumping dead bodies, he'd wanted to add.

He'd been round at her place for over an hour and had been reluctant to leave. Back in the flat with Daisy, he'd slumped down in front of the TV while she watched afternoon quiz shows. Why the hell was she watching quizzes when she was so dumb? He wondered how much of the knowledge was going in and how much was just sailing right over her head.

Thankfully his mobile had rung to relieve the tedium. It was Jamie ringing from London. Glenn left the living room so he could talk away from the sound of *The Chase*.

'Can we meet up?' Jamie asked him. 'I'm in a spot of bother.'

'Sure,' Glenn said. 'Anything to get out of here.'

So once again he'd told Daisy that he was going out, and once again she'd hardly batted an eyelid. Glenn had made the mile walk to Redgate station and caught a train to East Croydon, just a twenty minute ride away. He'd agreed to meet Jamie in a bar near the station that they'd met in several times before.

Jamie was already there when Glenn walked in, sitting at a table with a pint. He stood up and they had a hug, then Jamie went to the bar to buy him a pint as well.

When they were both sitting down Jamie said, 'I went to court yesterday and was charged with assault. Along with my so called friend Ray.'

Glenn sat there stunned, not sure if he'd heard right. Then Jamie told him the whole story about the busty barmaid and how Ray had attacked her and ripped her T-shirt down the front. Glenn could see his life flashing before his eyes, things that he'd done in the past, his first crimes, and now his son seemed to be going down that same route too. Glenn had never assaulted a woman though. You had to draw the line somewhere.

He sat there in depressed silence for half a minute and then said, 'Jesus, I'm such a bad example. You can be the new Mister Me.'

'What's that?' Jamie asked, puzzled.

'Some song I heard somewhere. About a gunfighter. The young gun on his trail shoots him and as the old gunfighter is dying he says, "You can be the new Mister Me." In other words, you can have my legacy and good luck with it. It's a good song. Damned if I can remember who sang it though.'

'I can look it up on the Internet,' Jamie said.

'Yeah. It will be on there for sure. Let me know who sang it. Hopefully you won't end up as bad as me though. When do you go to trial?'

Jamie shrugged. 'I don't know. A few months I guess. Maybe longer. These things can drag on forever.'

Glenn nodded. 'Well keep it under your hat. Don't tell the folks at Argos or you'll be out on your ear. It's amazing what you can get away with if you don't tell anyone.'

'No way am I going to tell them. I'm not stupid.'

Glenn decided to change the subject. 'I've just met another woman,' he said. 'And I think she might be the one.'

'I thought Daisy was the one,' Jamie said.

'No, she was just a piece of fluff. Today I spent about two hours with the woman next door. Her name's Angie. She can actually hold a conversation. *And* she's funny.'

Jamie shook his head. 'You don't widen your scope much do you? First a woman in your own building and then the one next door.'

'Well, why go travelling when something's on your doorstep?'

'So what's going to happen?'

'I don't know.'

Jamie took a sip of beer. 'Seeing as how you killed her husband, I would say you have no choice but to stay with Daisy. If you walk out the door she'll go straight to the police.'

'If she can find the police station,' Glenn smirked. 'My first instinct was not to touch her you know. You should always trust your first instincts.'

'Famous last words.'

'Looks like both of us are in a spot of bother.'

'Yeah. I don't know whose position I prefer.'

'Well, you've got *two* things to worry about,' Glenn said.

'What do you mean?'

'The assault and helping me with Vernon's body. At least I've only got the one thing.'

'Yeah but *you* murdered him. That far outweighs what I've done. I feel I'm being persecuted for just getting a feel of tit.'

Glenn looked around the bar. It was about half full, some office workers starting to drift in. Most of them were in their twenties and thirties, young guns with wallets full of easy cash, getting pissed each night and chatting up women, too naïve to see the disappointments that would surely lie ahead. Glenn still envied them though. It was better than his situation, waiting out time until he died.

'If I had a load of money,' he said, 'I would just disappear. Get out of this fucking country for good.'

'You're not the first to think that, and you won't be the last.'

'Have you never had that thought?'

'Not really. I'm still young and full of hope,' Jamie said with sarcasm. 'Or young, dumb, and full of cum.'

'Yeah. I'm old and numb and running out of cum.'

'But still putting it to the ladies.'

'And if you end up in jail *you'll* be putting it to the laddies.'

Jamie shook his head. 'No way will that happen to me. I'll defend my arse with my life.'

Glenn smiled. 'That's my boy. The new Mister Me.'

When they were on their second pint, Jamie came up with a plan that Glenn had to admit had promise and a certain flare to it. He said, 'I think I know a way we could get some quick money.'

Glenn raised his eyebrows.

'When I went to have a guitar lesson in Chiswick,' Jamie said, 'we were walking down the road and Jason told me about a film star who lives there. I looked her up on the Internet when I got home and she's been in lots of things. She must be loaded. How about we pay her a visit one day? See what money she has lying around the house.'

'What's her name?'

'Sara Shriver.'

Glenn thought for a few seconds. 'The name sounds familiar. Show me a picture.'

Jamie took out his smart phone and found a Shriver photo on the 'net. Glenn recognised her face. 'Jesus. She's in that cop show on ITV. I've watched it a few times. I think you might have struck gold. And you know where she lives?'

'I know the street. I don't know the exact house number.'

'But this Jason guy knows?'

'Yeah. He goes round to see her.'

'So we go and ask Jason and then go around to hers.'

'Could do. Would be fun seeing what's in her house. I've never been in a movie star's home before.'

'Probably not that much different. Except for the furniture and fittings.'

'And hopefully a large amount of cash hanging around. And jewellery. You're a bit of a jewellery expert.'

'Used to be.'

'I'm sure it wouldn't take you long to learn again.'

'Too right. It's something to think about,' Glenn said.

They'd stayed in the bar for four pints in total, then Glenn said he'd better get back to Daisy. He'd arrived home at eight o'clock, already feeling like a downtrodden married man, but at least he was half pissed. And what was the worst she could do, give him the silent treatment?

Now it was Thursday morning and Glenn was looking at the bedroom window and wishing he was next door with Angie. Looking back, if he'd carried on ignoring Daisy for another week then none of this would have happened. He'd still be single, Vernon would still be alive, and he could have chatted up Angie with no ties at all. He would have been like a pig in shit - instead of an ex-con in a load of shit.

He climbed out of bed, Daisy still deep in sleep. He went upstairs to the bathroom and then went back to his own room and slumped down on the bed. He could think better if he was away from Daisy. He thought about Angie again and once again his dick started getting hard. Then he thought about Sara Shriver and a house full of goodies. His dick got even harder.

## CHAPTER EIGHTEEN.

One week after his visit to Stoke Newington to see Gill, Jason still hadn't given Mary Ann a ring. Her phone number was burning a hole on his mobile list of contacts but he just didn't have the self confidence to ring, or even send a text. He just couldn't figure out why a stunning woman in her early thirties would want to go out with him. She was way out of his league.

Jason had been turned down by many women in the past, women who he'd thought at the time fancied him. He just wasn't a good judge of who liked him and who didn't. Was any man? Yes, probably some of them. Those smooth good looking bastards who could get off with any woman they chose, usually total bastards that women seemed to be attracted to. Jason's main weakness he had figured out, was that he was one of the good guys, and maybe some women found that a bit dull. He knew he was good husband material, but for a lover he was probably not the most exciting. It was something he couldn't change now. He was fifty-two after all. It was far too late to be changing his personal image and life outlook.

He heard the front doorbell ring. It was two in the afternoon. He didn't have another lesson for an hour or so.

He left the living room, walked into the communal front hall, and opened the door. He was surprised and very worried to find Jamie standing there, with an older, rough looking man by his side.

Jason forced a smile and said hello.

Jamie nodded and introduced the older man as his father. 'We were just in the area,' he added. 'Can we come in for a second?'

Jason looked at his watch. 'I've got a lesson soon.'

'This won't take long,' Jamie said. 'It's not about the text I sent you. It's about something else. Don't worry.'

Jason reluctantly said okay and held the door open for them. They didn't seem to be in an aggressive mood so what the hell. He was kind of interested to see what they wanted.

In the living room Jason didn't offer them a seat. He wanted to see exactly where this was going first. So they all stood just inside the door and Jamie said, 'We'd like to know where Sara Shriver lives. We want to go and visit her.'

Jason hadn't been expecting that at all. 'Why do you want to do that?'

'My dad's a big fan. When I told him about her he couldn't wait to come down.'

The older man nodded and said, 'That's right. I've seen a lot of her films.'

Jason nearly said, Well why don't you name a few then? He didn't believe them for a second. Instead he said, 'She's a very private woman. She won't want any fans just knocking on her door. I wouldn't know if she's in anyway.'

'Thought you might say that,' Jamie said. 'Don't worry. We won't tell her that you told us. There must be many local people who know where she lives. We'll just pretend we live around here. All my dad wants is an autograph.'

Jason thought about it again. They were both being quite friendly. And what would happen if he didn't give them Sara's number? Would they resort to violence? He decided the easiest way out was just to give them the house number.

'It's twenty-two,' he said. 'You know the street.'

'Great,' Jamie said. 'Twenty-two. We won't mention your name if she asks where we got it from.'

'I'd appreciate that,' Jason said.

'And don't worry about that other thing,' Jamie said. 'I was feeling in a bad mood.'

Jason wanted to ask just what was going on with that, if Jamie had been charged yet, but with his tough looking dad standing there it was probably better to just say nothing and nod. So that's what he did.

The older man reached out a hand and Jason shook it. He was expecting a rough hand to go with the face but his skin was surprisingly soft. Not a manual worker for sure.

They said goodbye and Jason let them out.

Back in the living room Jason wondered whether he should ring Sara and warn her, but that would just put him in her bad books for telling the two ruffians where she lived. Hopefully she would be out, no one would answer the doorbell and that would be the end of that. Jason picked up his guitar and tried to forget about it.

\*\*\*

Up in the spare room of number twenty-two, Sara Shriver had just had another session with Rick Clayburn. A session without guitars that is, though she had been strumming on something else and Rick had almost been singing another tune.

'That was nice,' she said, catching her breath. 'Seems like you had a lot of extra energy today.'

Rick nodded, some sweat forming on his forehead. 'Well I haven't seen you for a few days. I've been storing it all up.'

'So I noticed. I don't know where it all comes from. It's almost like magic.'

'Yeah,' Rick said. 'It is pretty magical. Especially for me.' He grinned at her.

The front doorbell rang and Sara said, 'Damn, who the hell could that be?'

'Jason maybe?' Rick said.

'No, he isn't due round.'

Sara climbed out of bed and grabbed a flimsy white silk dressing gown. She walked out of the room, across the landing, and into one of the kid's bedrooms at the front of the house. She went to the window and looked down at the front door. Two men were standing there, one young and one old, and she didn't recognise either of them.

She went back to the bedroom, took off the dressing gown and climbed back into bed. 'Just a couple of builders I think. Probably trying to sell their amazing roof work or something.'

'Cowboy builders,' Rick said. 'Full of their cowboy dreams. Just what you don't need.'

'Come to rip off the rich and famous movie star.'

'Little do they know.'

'Indeed.'

'Probably time to get up anyway,' Rick said. 'I've got a lesson later.'

\*\*\*

Glenn looked at Jamie and said, 'Let's try the back door.'

Number 22 was the last house on the street so it was no problem walking into the back garden. Down the side of the house, through a gate, and then they were there. Glenn walked over to the back door, turned the knob, and in they went.

They stood in a large kitchen listening for sounds but all was quiet. Then they heard a few voices coming from upstairs and a minute later someone was coming down. Glenn and Jamie were now in the front hall so they stepped to the left and hid in a room that was full of musical instruments. Someone then walked right past the room and headed for the kitchen.

Using hand signals Glenn told Jamie to stand still and be quiet. But Jamie was standing right next to a guitar that was sitting on a stand and he brushed it by mistake with his left hand. His fingers hit the strings and made a sound that seemed pretty loud to Glenn. He gave his son a dirty look and waited.

Sure enough, the sound attracted someone, and that someone walked straight into the room and saw them both standing there. It was Sara Shriver.

\*\*\*

Sara couldn't believe what she was seeing. The two builders that she'd just seen outside were now in her living room. What the hell was going on? She was still only wearing her white silk nightgown, nothing on underneath, so she felt extremely vulnerable.

'Who the hell are you?' she said. 'And what are you doing in my living room?'

'We've come to rob you,' the older man said. 'So just do as you're told and nothing will happen.'

And then the younger man was right behind her and had his arms around her holding on tight. Sara struggled to get free but couldn't so she shouted as loud as possible, 'Rick! Come down here quick!'

\*\*\*

Upstairs in the bedroom Rick heard Sara's cry and wondered if she was playing a game or being serious. He climbed out of bed, not rushing at all, and put on his boxer shorts. He was about to go downstairs but then thought he'd better put some clothes on in case someone else was down there as well. So he slipped on his jeans and T-shirt and started padding down the stairs.

The first room he came to was the music room so he stepped in there expecting to see Sara sprawled out on the sofa in a provocative pose. He didn't have time to see much of anything though, because a big fist came out of nowhere and smashed him in the face. He fell to the floor like he'd been hit by a train.

\*\*\*

Sara screamed as Rick hit the floor, blood coming out of his nose. The younger man was holding her behind the door, while the older one took care of Rick. He grabbed some guitar leads and started tying him up, first his hands behind his back and then his legs.

The younger man was still holding Sara's arms from behind and in the struggle her dressing gown had now come undone. When the older man had finished with Rick he got up off the floor and looked at her and smiled.

'Jesus,' he said. 'You are one beautiful woman.'

Then he walked right up to her, pulled her dressing gown wide open, and had a good long look. Then he reached up a hand and started fondling her breasts.

\*\*\*

Jamie couldn't believe what he was seeing, his old man fondling a half naked woman right there in front of him. He wanted to see what his dad was seeing too. This film star was a looker and he wanted to see her naked. So he let go of her arms and came around to the front.

He almost had to catch his breath. The woman had nice sized breasts and a dark patch of neatly trimmed hair between her legs. And she was standing there watching the two of them, almost as if she didn't mind.

Jamie nudged his father out of the way and started groping her breasts as well.

\*\*\*

Sara was trying to act as if it was all some nasty scene from a violent thriller. She'd acted scenes in the past where the lead actor, or maybe someone not so lead, was pawing at her breasts, even one rape scene in a car many years ago when she was in her twenties. She was closing the men out of her mind as their hands went all over her, but when the older man reached down for her bush, that's when she decided she'd had enough. She reached behind her and grabbed a microphone stand and swung it round hard, hitting the older man on the side of his head.

Both men backed away and looked at her. The older man was stunned and she thought he might fall over. Or come back and kill her. She was swinging the stand wildly in front of her now and telling them to get the hell away from her. Then she started shouting and screaming as loud as she could and much to her surprise the two men ran out of the room, down the hall, and out of the front door.

Sara went to the door and locked it behind them, then went to the back door and locked that as well. Then, after making sure that Rick was still breathing, she went upstairs to put on some clothes.

When she was dressed, she picked up the bedside phone with shaking hands and called the police. Then she went back downstairs to start untying Rick.

## CHAPTER NINETEEN.

Jamie and Glenn Swell ran to the corner of the street and then turned left. Jamie had to help his dad along as he was a little dazed from the swipe to his head by the microphone stand. Jamie was still trying to get the image of the naked Sara Shriver out of his head. He wished he'd had time to take a few photos, but at least he could store the naked image in his wank bank for later. He had never seen such a nice looking woman before. She was even better looking than the barmaid Gill.

Jamie didn't really know where he was leading his father, and as they slowed to a walk he realised that they were in fact heading in the direction of Jason's place once again. It might be a good place to hide for a while, so he led his father there and rang the front doorbell.

Jason took several minutes and a couple of more rings to open the door. He looked at the two of them with a worried expression and Jamie asked if they could come inside.

'Why do you want to come in this time?' Jason asked.

'My dad's just been hit on the head,' Jamie said. 'He might be concussed.'

'Hit on the head by who?' Jason asked.

'I'll tell you when you let us in,' Jamie said, and Jason reluctantly stood aside.

\*\*\*

Jason was cursing his luck. He thought he'd got rid of these two half an hour ago and now here they were right back in his living room. And sitting themselves down on the sofa too.

Jason went to the kitchen to fetch a glass of water for Jamie's dad who looked a bit out of it, then sat in a chair and watched while he drank. 'So what happened?' he asked Jamie.

'We were walking down the road and these two Poles came up to us,' Jamie said. 'They asked us for some money and we ended up in a fight. Dad got hit on the head by one of them.'

Jason nodded. It sounded feasible. There were a lot of Poles in the Chiswick and Acton area and a lot of them were out of work. He often saw them in the parks drinking cans of beer at ten in the morning.

'So you didn't get to see Sara then?' he asked.

Jamie shook his head. 'Didn't get that far. It seems like a silly idea now. I think we'll just go home.'

'Do you want me to call the police?'

'About what?'

'About the attack by the Poles.'

Jamie shook his head. 'No. They won't find them. And the police are the last people I want to see at the moment.'

Jason looked at his watch. He had another lesson soon and he would prefer it if these two weren't there. Though Jamie seemed friendly enough, his rough looking father somehow seemed even more scary with the dazed look on his face.

'I'll make you a cup of tea,' Jason said. 'But I've got a lesson at three so you'll have to push off. That's unless you don't want to ring for an ambulance or anything.'

'No that's fine,' Jamie said, looking at his silent father. 'A cup of tea might do the trick. Have you got any biscuits?'

Jason left the room and busied himself in the kitchen, glad to be away from them for a few minutes to think. He cursed the day he had given Jamie his business card. He would have to be more careful in the future; you just didn't know who your clients could turn out to be.

He made a pot of tea and put it on a tray, along with three mugs, a container of milk, and a packet of biscuits. But when he arrived back in the living room only Jamie was sitting there. Jason put the tray down on the coffee table and said, 'Where's your dad disappeared to?'

Then he felt an arm going around his neck and he was being dragged backwards by a very strong man and being dumped into a chair. The two men were on him quickly, tying him up with guitar leads and Jason could do nothing about it no matter how hard he struggled. Eventually he gave in and let them tie him up.

'What was the point of that?' he said angrily when the two men had finished. They were standing in front of him grinning.

'We didn't come here for rest and recuperation,' Jamie said. 'We came for money.'

The older man nodded. 'That's why we went to the film star's house. And as we left empty handed we thought we'd come here and fleece you instead.'

Jason nodded. He should have suspected that from the start. 'You didn't harm Sara did you?' he said.

The two men looked at each other and grinned again. 'I wouldn't say harmed,' the older man said. 'But we certainly got an eyeful.'

Jason didn't really know what they meant by that. He hoped that Sara was all right.

'What we really want is your bank cards,' Jamie said. 'And your pin number. We're going to take some money out of your account. Otherwise our whole trip will have been wasted.'

Jason shook his head. 'Good luck with that. You can both go fuck yourselves.'

The older man stepped behind him and started pulling Jason's right arm right up behind his back. Jason cried out in pain and the man let his arm back down again.

'Want to try that again?' Jamie asked. 'Or do you just want to hand over your cards?'

Jason was starting to sweat, reminded of the time in Woodvale when Phil Gator had tied him up and then broken his right thumb. He wondered if the same thing was about to happen. It had taken him months before he was able to play the guitar again.

'Okay,' he said. 'I only have two cards. There're in my wallet. Try my coat on the door.'

Jamie went over to Jason's coat that was hanging on the living room door and started going through the pockets. He came out with Jason's wallet, opened it up, and found a blue Visa card and a red one for Santander, and put them both in his jeans pocket. He tossed the wallet at the coffee table. It missed and landed on the floor at Jason's feet.

'Right, now we need the pin numbers,' Jamie said.

'The year of my birth,' Jason said. '1961. They're both the same.'

'Easy to remember,' Jamie's father said.

'And we want a guitar too,' Jamie said. 'The police will be looking for two men, but they won't be expecting one of them to be carrying a guitar. Where's that expensive one you told me about?'

Jason felt a sickness in his stomach. He'd shown Jamie his £2,000 Martin D-28 when he'd had his guitar lesson, had even let him hold it for a few minutes. It was virtually irreplaceable though it was insured.

'It's over by the door,' he said faintly. 'In the guitar case.'

Jamie looked over and saw it. 'Great. We'll take it on the way out. You can kiss your axe goodbye.'

His father looked at him puzzled.

'Axe is another name for guitar,' Jamie explained.

His dad nodded. 'Good one son.'

Then Jamie looked back at Jason. 'There is just one more thing.'

He walked behind Jason and put his head right next to his face. 'I don't like grasses,' he said quietly, 'and I really don't appreciate that you told the police about me.'

Jason looked up at Jamie's dad who was watching the scene with a smile on his face. Then Jason felt Jamie's hands on his and then he was grabbing him by the fingers and twisting them. Jason knew what was going to happen, because it had happened to him before. These criminals just didn't have any imagination. He heard the snap of his middle finger and then felt a shooting pain going right up his arm. He shouted out once again, tears coming into his eyes, and then Jamie was standing in front of him.

'That'll stop you from playing the guitar for a while, guitar man.'

And then the two of them left, taking the two grand Martin on their way out.

\*\*\*

When the police and ambulance arrived, Rick Clayburn was sitting on a chair and conscious, socks now on his feet so it didn't look like he'd just tumbled out of bed. Sara told the police that they'd both been upstairs when the intruders had arrived. She didn't tell them that she'd only been wearing a dressing gown. She'd made sure the spare room looked normal but the police never ventured upstairs.

Sara told them how she'd been molested, but told them she was wearing jeans and blouse at the time. She told the plainclothes Detective in as much detail as she could remember. A couple of paramedics checked Rick over and then walked him out of the room and into an ambulance. He had to go to hospital for a precautionary scan.

'Can you describe the two men?' the Detective asked.

Sara was sitting on a chair, slippers on her feet.

'The younger one was about twenty-five. Short brown hair, muscle-bound arms. About five feet ten. The older one was about fifty-five. Craggy face. Grey hair. He looked like a builder. Slightly shorter. Both were wearing jeans. The old guy had a blue shirt on and the younger one was wearing a grey T-shirt.'

The Detective turned to his left and his partner said, 'I'm on it,' and then disappeared.

'We'll see if we can pick them up right now,' the Detective said. 'They might still be around.'

Sara chatted some more with the Detective and he showed some interest in her TV and music work. She told him that both were going okay. Then she gave him one of her CDs from a pile sitting on the floor.

'We'll try and keep this out of the papers,' he said, staring down at the front cover of her CD, the photo showing too much of her cleavage, a photo she'd regretted ever since.

Sara nodded. 'That would be preferable.'

She was well known in the area and it would probably make the national news before she knew it. She wondered if that was a bad thing. Probably not. It would get her name into the limelight for a few days and it might even lead to more work. All publicity was good publicity after all. She remembered the case of singer Joss Stone, those two men who'd been caught who were going to kidnap or murder her, Sara couldn't remember the exact details. Joss's name had been all over the TV then, a bizarre and gruesome case. It put Joss back in the limelight for a while. Maybe her sales had improved after?

Sara's husband David arrived on the scene after half an hour, leaving work early after she'd phoned him. He walked into the living room and gave her a hug and a concerned look.

'Have you any idea who they were?' he asked. Sara shook her head. Then to the policeman, 'You're going to find these two I hope?' Trying to sound forceful but only managing to sound a little pathetic.

The Detective shrugged. 'We'll do the best we can. But they might have just vanished into thin air. We've got some men out now.'

David asked about Rick and Sara told him he was okay. He was used to Rick being around so wouldn't think anything unusual was going on. They left the living room and went to the kitchen for a glass of wine while the fingerprint men went to work.

\*\*\*

After leaving Jason's place, Jamie and his dad headed straight for Turnham Green station, Jamie carrying Jason's heavy guitar over his shoulder as camouflage. They also looked for a cash machine but couldn't see any around. They had to stop and ask someone and were pointed down towards the end of the road.

'Fucking hell,' Glenn grumbled. 'Rich part of town and the cash machine's two hundred yards away.'

'Do you want to risk it or just go home?' Jamie asked.

'Let's risk it.'

So they walked off down the street, crossed Chiswick High Road, and queued up at the cash machine where there were four people in front of them. Jamie withdrew the highest amount possible, three hundred pounds.

'That's not going to last long,' his father moaned.

'When we get back to central London we'll withdraw at every machine we come to,' Jamie said. 'Until it stops working.'

'Let's hope that Jason doesn't escape from his chair for the next hour then,' his father said.

Once on the tube his father started to relax, seemingly recovered now from the blow to his head.

Jamie hadn't realised that the actress had hit him so hard. Or maybe his dad wasn't as tough as he thought he was. Or maybe he was just getting old. Jamie gave him a bottle of Lucozade and a Lion bar that he'd bought at the station, and his father sat quietly nibbling on his little reviving feast.

The trip hadn't been a complete waste of time and if they could withdraw some more money quickly it would be a few hours well spent. It hadn't been much of a plan really, going to a film star's house and trying to get money out of her. What did they expect - a safe filled with jewellery and used bank notes? That was the kind of thing that would only happen in *Columbo* or some other TV mystery. But it had been an adventure of sorts, and they'd seen the film star naked. That would be something to laugh about in the years ahead.

But by the time the train had left the over ground section and entered the dark tunnels, Jamie had decided once again that he should really be spending less time with his father. This was the second time they'd been involved in a serious crime in the space of just a few weeks. They obviously brought out the worst in each other. He'd be better off lying low at Argos and not going down to Redgate for a few months, or even meeting up in Croydon. That would be the best for both of them.

When the train reached Embankment station, his father suggested they go for a drink together. 'Let's go down to one of the boats,' he said. 'A good way to end the day.'

'Aren't you forgetting something?' Jamie said.

His father gave him a puzzled look. Maybe he hadn't recovered from the blow to his head after all.

'The cash machines,' Jamie said quietly. They were standing at Embankment station, the beginnings of rush hour crowds swirling around them.

His father nodded. 'Oh yeah. Let's forget about the boat. We'll have a drink in Covent Garden instead.'

Jamie nodded. Yes, he really would have to see less of his dad from now on – his brain didn't seem to be working anymore. They headed out of the station and up the hill towards Charing Cross looking for the first cash machine to hit.

# CHAPTER TWENTY.

Jason remained in his chair with the pain unbearable in his right hand. He wondered how long his middle finger would take to heal. And more importantly, would it screw up his guitar playing for good? The middle finger was the most important one for finger-picking. He now had two digits on his right hand that had been broken by petty criminals. It just wasn't fair. What had he done to deserve all this?

He tried to loosen the guitar leads that were holding his hands behind the back of the chair but they just wouldn't budge. Luckily his feet hadn't been tied so he managed to rock himself forwards and stand up so he could then shuffle around the room with the chair on his back like a disfigured tortoise. But where could he shuffle to? He couldn't get out of the flat because of the round doorknob. If it had been a lever type he could have just kicked it open then sat in the front hall waiting for someone to come along. So his only plan was to sit by the door and when he heard footsteps on the other side, kick the door hard and shout for help.

So he sat there and waited.

For what seemed like an age.

His doorbell rang at three o'clock when his next lesson arrived. Jason pictured the teenage girl called Jemima standing outside with her classical guitar, cussing him for not being there. She was a sweet looking girl with curly hair, one of his favourite pupils. But there wasn't much he could do about it.

Then he heard his mobile ringing, which was probably Jemima ringing from outside to see where he was. He'd call her later and apologise, give her next lesson for free. That's if he could ever give another lesson with a broken finger.

After about thirty minutes he heard someone coming along so he kicked at the door with both feet and started shouting Help! which was the only word he could think of. The person on the other side of the door then called back Hello, who is it?

Jason recognised the voice of one of the men who lived upstairs, a Scandinavian called Bo. Jason shouted some more to him and eventually the door knob turned and Bo was standing there.

'I've been attacked and robbed,' Jason said to him, feeling like he might break down in tears. 'Can you untie me? They've broken one of my fingers.'

Bo looked suitably shocked and went behind Jason to set him free. He was a large strong looking man with a bit of a beer gut. Then he took his mobile out of his pocket and rang for the police and an ambulance.

While they were waiting Jason got Bo to ring Visa and Santander so he could put a stop on both of his cards. He wondered how much money had been withdrawn in the last hour or so. He had no idea what the limit was on drawing money out in one day.

He was regretting giving Jamie and his dad his pin number. He could have given them a false one, 1962 instead of 1961 for instance. Why on earth had he told them the truth? Probably because he'd been scared of them returning. Also because he wasn't streetwise enough and he was too honest. He usually told the truth when asked something. That was one of his weaknesses. And surely he'd get all the money back anyway? He hoped so. Otherwise he'd really be in the shit.

But much worse than that was the thought of his stolen Martin. It was his constant companion and now it was gone. The thought of not seeing it again was giving him a hollow feeling in his stomach like someone had just ripped his guts out. He could always buy another one with the insurance money but it wouldn't be the same. You couldn't replace history.

He looked down at his right hand, the middle finger sticking out in the wrong direction. Then Bo came in from the kitchen carrying some whisky in a glass. Jason knocked it back in one and hoped it would lessen the pain.

\*\*\*

When he arrived home at ten in the evening, Glenn was half-drunk from the booze he'd had with Jamie. They'd walked to Covent Garden from Embankment, withdrawn another £300 from a cash machine, then had the card eaten by the next cash machine a few minutes later. So their total of £600 was all they'd acquired from their trip to Chiswick. That and a carrier bag each full of booze.

After the Santander card had disappeared they'd hurried to the first off-licence they could find and bought some expensive booze on Jason's Visa. Twelve bottles of spirits in all, six each. Expensive malts, brandy and vodka. Glenn had also bought a bottle of Bailey's for Daisy. She loved the creamy stuff, had told him the other day that it reminded her of drinking his spunk. Such a classy woman. If his spunk really tasted of Bailey's maybe he could market himself as some kind of exotic gigolo. He would really need a second opinion though. Maybe Angie would be willing to help.

He unlocked the front door and walked in quietly. Hopefully Daisy would be in bed so he wouldn't have to talk to her, tell her where he'd been. He crept upstairs and found her in the living room, wide awake, watching TV as usual.

He said hello and sat down on the edge of her armchair. Reached in the carrier bag and brought out the bottle of Bailey's. 'I bought you this,' he said. 'Been with Jamie all day in London.'

Daisy took the bottle and looked at it.

'Fancy a drink?' he asked, and she nodded like a mute animal.

Glenn went back to the kitchen with the carrier and set it on the table. He took out a bottle of Jack Daniel's and poured himself a large shot. Then he took the wad of cash from his pocket, about £280, and laid it there as well. He poured a Bailey's for Daisy and carried the drinks back to the living room.

Slumping down on the sofa he wished it was Angie sitting across from him. At least he'd have some decent conversation and a laugh. He looked at the TV. Daisy was watching something about a serial killer in the US. It was actually quite interesting so he sat there and watched. After ten minutes he lay down on the sofa with his whisky glass on his chest. After another ten minutes he was fast asleep.

***

They kept Rick Clayburn in hospital overnight for observation. He'd been punched pretty hard and he was still feeling drowsy.

Sara Shriver sat beside his bed as Rick nibbled on some grapes. He had a large swelling on the side of his right cheek. She'd told him in detail about how the two men had felt her up. Then wished she hadn't. Rick started getting angry and stress was the last thing he needed.

Her mobile started buzzing in her bag so she took it out and answered. It was Jason. He told her that he was in Hammersmith Hospital with a broken finger, broken by a couple of intruders.

'That's a coincidence,' Sara said. 'Because I'm in Hammersmith Hospital as well. With Rick.'

She told him what had happened while Rick lay there looking at her. She offered to go and visit Jason as well but he said not to bother. The hospital was so big he doubted she'd be able to find him. He'd catch a bus home when they'd fixed him up.

She turned off her mobile and told Rick about Jason.

'That's a coincidence,' he said. 'Both of us being attacked by nutters on the same day.'

'It is,' Sara said. 'Maybe someone's out to demolish our successful group.'

Rick grinned. 'It's a conspiracy by other well known bands. They see us as a threat. It's probably the Arctic Monkeys and Oasis who arranged the whole thing.'

'Oasis don't exist anymore do they?'

'Just testing you,' Rick said. 'Beady Eye. That's what they're called now. Half of them anyway.'

'I should have asked Jason what his attackers looked like. Maybe they were the same people.'

'I would very much doubt that. Must just be a coincidence.'

'Poor guy won't be able to play guitar for a while.'

'Yeah, that really sucks. I would have liked him in the band to do a bit of picking and backing vocals. We'll cheer him up by putting three of his songs on the CD.'

'By the time the CD gets done maybe he'll be all right,' Sara said. 'I really don't know how long a broken finger takes to heal.'

'Me neither. Probably depends on what kind of a break it is. Clean or complicated.'

Sara looked around at the other people in the ward, about a dozen beds altogether. Some of them were looking over, recognising her from the TV. One of the nurses had already asked for her autograph. Sara had obliged, writing on a piece of hospital stationery.

'Did David suspect anything?' Rick asked.

Sara shook her head. 'He never does. He lives in his own little business world. Sometimes I wonder if he'd mind even if he knew.'

Rick nodded. 'It's at times like this that you start to wonder. About the future and everything. Where it's all going to lead.'

Sara nodded. 'I know. It makes you think about what's really important. What you really want from life.'

'And what do you really want from life?'

Sara reached over and took his hand. 'That's the big question, isn't it?'

\*\*\*

Sitting in her armchair, sipping her Bailey's, Daisy watched Glenn sleeping. Since he'd arrived home a lump had appeared on his forehead without him noticing. She wondered where he'd got that from. He must have been involved in a bar fight or something.

She stood up slowly and walked down to the kitchen. On the table she found a large amount of cash and six bottles of alcohol. She had no idea where all that had appeared from so obviously Glenn had been up to no good. The man was obviously a liability, always getting himself into trouble. And now he was even trying to chat up Angie next door. Daisy had watched them both from the living room window talking in the street.

She left the kitchen and walked back up the two steps into the bedroom, took one of the pillows off the bed and went into the living room.

Glenn was still lying there, out cold in his drunken stupor. She walked over to him and put the pillow down over his head. Then she leaned over him and pushed down hard.

Daisy had strong arms from all her fights with Vernon. He liked to rough her up before they had sex and he liked her to fight back. Then he liked to slap her around the head which was the main reason why her face was always swollen. Then Vernon told the few people they came into contact with that it was the drugs. Daisy knew different though. It was nothing to do with the drugs at all.

She also had strong arms from the weights Vernon kept underneath their bed. When he was out she would bring a chair into the bedroom and have hourly sessions with the radio on, sitting there in the chair doing repetitions, up and down, up and down, getting her arms strong for whatever conflict was bound to happen eventually. But the conflict with Vernon had never materialized because she'd managed to manoeuvre Glenn into that position instead, first seducing him and then telling Vernon all about it so they would have their punch up, their showdown, up in Glenn's bedroom.

The drugs were all an act. Vernon had thought she was taking about ten pills a day for her various 'women's problems' but really she was flushing them down the toilet. Glenn had thought the same too. Poor deluded men, thinking they had a poor weak woman to look after, a woman they could screw any time they liked and then cast aside.

She pushed down harder on the pillow and Glenn struggled a little, not as much as she'd imagined he would, and after five minutes he didn't move any more. She lifted the pillow off and felt for a pulse on his neck. He seemed to be dead.

She went back to her armchair and slumped down, quite tired from the exertion. She'd sit there a while just to make sure Glenn didn't start breathing again. If he did she'd just smother him a second time. Then in the morning she could think about what to do with his body, and then make plans for the rest of her life. She deserved one after all. Just like everyone else.

## CHAPTER TWENTY-ONE.

Back home in the early evening - with his right hand bandaged so all his fingers were in a straight line and couldn't move - Jason wondered where his life would lead him now. He wouldn't be able to play the guitar for a few months that was for sure, and when he was able to move his fingers again would finger-picking even be possible? Maybe he would just end up strumming his guitar with his thumb like Johnny Cash used to. It was a thought he couldn't really bear thinking about. He loved to fingerpick. He believed his style set him apart from all the other guitarists around. Not many people even knew how to fingerpick these days. His years of experience separated him from the rest.

Maybe he would end up like Joe Strummer of The Clash, who'd got his nickname because he wasn't much good on the guitar, just a strummer. Maybe he could steal his name now that Strummer was dead. Jason Strummer. Somehow it didn't have the same ring to it.

His mobile rang on the coffee table and he picked it up. It was Gill.

'Hey,' she said. 'How are things with you?'

Jason told her what had happened and Gill was silent with shock. Then she said, 'I just can't believe that guy. Someone has to do something about him. He's like a dickhead out of control.'

Jason couldn't disagree with that. A dickhead out of control. It almost made him laugh.

'Why don't you come for lunch tomorrow,' Gill said. 'I've got someone I'd like you to meet. That's if you're feeling up to it of course.'

Jason thought about it for a second. He could probably manage travelling with one hand. And maybe he would get to see Mary Ann again. So he agreed to meet Gill and hung up.

He spent the rest of the evening sitting in front of the TV catching up on DVDs he hadn't watched. *Six Feet Under* and *Breaking Bad*. He also cancelled the next day's lessons and rang the girl Jemima to apologise for missing her lesson. He told them that he'd broken his finger in a fall. He felt too embarrassed to tell them the truth. He drank half a bottle of wine – thankful for the screw top now that he only had one hand – and ate a microwave lasagne. How would he even be able to cook anymore? He'd have to eat junk food for the foreseeable future. After two months of that he'd be looking like Mr Blobby.

Even getting ready for bed was a problem. Getting out of his jeans and even worse, his pullover and shirt. He slumped into bed feeling exhausted by the effort.

Then he started worrying about how he would earn enough money over the coming months. You didn't get sick pay when you were self-employed. Maybe he could get some kind of benefits off the council. He would have to check it out tomorrow.

\*\*\*

In the morning he struggled out of bed and made himself tea and toast, then washed down a couple of painkillers. His hand was still hurting and he wondered whether he'd slept on it during the night. Then he had the difficult task of showering without getting his hand wet. Then having a crap. He had to wipe his arse with his left hand, and even that seemingly simple task was a little bit awkward. But he'd have to get used to it. No one else was going to do it for him.

He left the house at twelve and walked over to South Acton over ground station. He had his kindle with him so he could read with one hand. Reading a paperback would have been too difficult. He hadn't used his kindle for a few months and found about ten classics on there that he hadn't started: *The Three Musketeers*, *Tess of the D'Urbervilles*, even *War and Peace*, to name but a few. He wondered how much room the latter was taking up. Probably very little. He clicked to page one of the Tolstoy tome and started reading.

By the time he arrived at Dalston Kingsland he'd read several hundred kindle pages which was probably about ten in a real book. Not too bad. He turned the kindle off and left the train, walked up the stairs to the street and waited for a bus.

When he arrived at Gill's house twenty-five minutes later he was wondering who her mystery guest would be, hoping it might be Mary Ann. He rang the doorbell and once again heard the loud barking of Santini and saw the dog's head as it ran towards the door. Then Gill appeared and let him in.

She gave him a big hug and looked at his bandaged hand, then led him through the house and down to the kitchen. Sitting at the table was a muscle bound man, very tanned with short brown hair, wearing a tight blue T-shirt. When he stood up Jason guessed his height at about six feet. He was broad in the shoulders, like he pumped iron everyday, and his legs were as thick as tree trunks.

Gill said, 'This is Lance Boyle. The man who you thought had a funny name?'

Jason laughed uncomfortably and held out his left hand. Lance Boyle smiled at him.

\*\*\*

Downstairs in the Argos storeroom, the day after his jaunt to Chiswick, Jamie was called to the manager's office to take a phone call. The manager was an Indian guy called Siva who Jamie struggled to understand at times, his English wasn't very clear. He gestured towards the phone on the desk and Jamie picked it up. He said hello and it was a woman's voice on the other end that he didn't recognise.

'This is Daisy,' the woman said. 'Your father's friend.'

'Hi,' Jamie said, then didn't know what else to say. He'd hardly spoken ten words to her the last time they'd met.

'Your father died last night,' Daisy told him in an emotionless robotic voice. 'A heart attack while he was watching TV.'

Jamie grabbed a chair and sat down. 'You're kidding me,' he said. 'Tell me you're not being serious.'

'I'm being serious,' Daisy said. 'And I want you to come down here straightaway. We need to talk. His body is still here.'

Jamie was confused. 'You mean you haven't rung the police yet? Or an ambulance?'

'No,' Daisy said. 'It's too risky. We have to talk first. Can you come down?'

Jamie looked across the room at Siva who was sitting at his desk entering figures on to a computer, trying hard not to listen in. Jamie told Daisy to hang on then asked Siva if he could take the rest of the day off. He told him that his father had just died. Siva said sure, looking suitably sympathetic, then went back to his computer.

'I'll leave right now,' Jamie said into the phone. 'I'll be there in an hour and a half or so. Maybe longer.'

Daisy said fine and rang off. Jamie looked at his watch. It was only ten past ten.

He said goodbye to Siva, locked his uniform up in his locker, and went up to the street level in the lift. He walked down Camden High Street in a daze, not really sure what he was feeling. Maybe his dad had been affected by that blow to his head. Maybe they had drunk too much booze afterwards, or maybe it was a combination of the drink and the excitement. He really didn't have a clue.

He walked all the way to Warren Street tube, a good fifteen minutes, and caught the Underground to Victoria station. He really needed a drink but didn't want to face Daisy half-cut. He wondered why she hadn't called the cops. It all sounded a little suspicious.

At Victoria station the need for alcohol was too great so he bought a couple of small bottles of wine for the train ride, plus a ham salad roll, then bought his ticket at a machine. On the train ride he stared out of the window, drinking and eating, and feeling a little better.

Much to his amazement, Daisy was waiting for him at Redgate station, standing there at the ticket barriers by the main entrance. She looked different somehow, quite attractive, and Jamie wondered if maybe she wanted to shag him as well, get a father and son notch on her belt. But did women really think that way about sex? He was damned if he knew.

She held out her hand for him to shake, all very formal, and told him she had a car waiting. When they walked into the car park Jamie saw that it was the same car that he and his father had used to dispose of Vernon's body, the red Polo. He was amazed that Daisy could drive. He had presumed she was too zombie-like to get anything like that together.

She drove him back to her place with minimal conversation. Jamie wasn't looking forward to seeing his dad's dead body. He was wishing that Daisy had just called the cops to clear it away instead.

She parked neatly in the street outside and led him upstairs to the first floor and the living room. There was a body on the sofa with a blanket covering it, two feet poking out of the end. The windows were open to get rid of any smells there might be. Daisy pulled the blanket back and sure enough, there was his dad, as dead as dead can be, his mouth wide open, his eyes shut.

Jamie didn't know how he was meant to react. Was Daisy expecting him to crumple to the floor in tears? Instead he said, 'So what happens now?'

Daisy dropped the blanket back over his dad's face, and led him to the kitchen where he sat down at the table while she made some tea. Then she took some Bakewell Tart out of a cupboard and cut him a slice. It had white icing on the top and a jam layer underneath. Jamie took a bite, feeling a little guilty.

Daisy set a cup of tea in front of him then said, 'Or maybe you'd prefer something stronger.'

Jamie looked up at her and said, 'Like what?'

She reached down to another cupboard and came out with a bottle of Glenfiddich, the very same bottle that his dad had bought yesterday in Covent Garden. Jamie nodded and said, 'That would hit the spot.'

Daisy poured them both a shot and they toasted his father. This Daisy was full of surprises. He really started to wonder whether he could shag her. She was probably only about ten years older than him.

Daisy said, 'I didn't ring the police because how would I explain why Glenn was in my living room watching TV? And how would I explain where my husband is? It's just too complicated.'

Jamie nodded. 'I can see that.'

'At first I was thinking maybe you and I could carry him back upstairs to his room so it would look like he'd died up there. But then I thought, the police would still be asking questions about Vernon and where he was. It's just too risky. Risky not only for me but for you too.'

'Why for me?' Jamie asked, not really seeing where this was going.

'Because you helped to get rid of Vernon's body. You would be implicated as well. We would both be in trouble.'

*Implicated.* This Daisy knew some long words after all. Jamie nodded and reached for some more Glenfiddich. 'So what do you have in mind?'

'The safest thing for us both would be to get rid of your father's body.'

Jamie nearly choked as he took a sip of his malt. 'You must be joking. I want to give my father a decent burial.'

'That's not possible,' Daisy said, giving him a cold look. 'As I just said, it wouldn't be good for either of us. We have to make him disappear. Maybe you can take him to where you buried Vernon. I'm sure they'll be very happy together.'

Jamie looked at her. Obviously his dad hadn't told her about Vernon's so called burial, being thrown off the edge of Fuller's Earth into the quarry. He really didn't want to do the same with his dad. And who the hell would help him anyway? He couldn't do it on his own.

'I wouldn't be able to carry his body,' he said, trying to wriggle out of the situation. 'Who's going to help me? You?'

Daisy shook her head. 'No, not me. I don't want to be involved. Isn't there someone else who could help you? Don't you have a partner in crime?'

Jamie knew exactly who she meant. Obviously his dad had told her all about his upcoming court appearance with Ray Lane. 'You mean my friend Ray?'

Daisy nodded. 'If that's what his name is.'

Jamie had to smile. She'd worked the whole thing out already and was way ahead of him. Yes Ray could help him all right. A little payback for getting him into trouble in the first place with the barmaid.

He took his mobile out of his pocket and said, 'I'll call him right away.'

## CHAPTER TWENTY-TWO.

'So what brings you to London?' Jason asked Lance.

The three of them were sitting at Gill's kitchen table, Lance drinking a bottle of beer, Jason and Gill on white wine.

'I'm on my way to France,' Lance said. 'I've got a runaway drug dealer to pick up and take back to California. Then Gill told me about her problems and I wondered if maybe I could help her out. I thought I'd stop off en route. And I see you've had some problems as well.' He nodded at Jason's hand.

'Yeah. The same guy has been hassling us both. It's all getting out of control.'

'Well, I think I can do something about it. I know where the guy lives. I can put a scare into him.'

'How do you know where he lives?' Jason asked.

'I've got contacts in the police. All it took was one phone call.'

Jason was impressed. 'So you're going to go round and rough him up a bit?'

'Sort of. Probably best if you don't know.'

Jason nodded. 'So how did you get into this business?'

'I was a cop for fifteen years but getting a little bored with it. In a small town in Arizona. I took a vacation in Vegas one summer and met a guy who was doing what I'm doing now. He was getting old and wanted to retire. Needed someone to take over his business. He was sick of all the flying around. So

I went on a few trips with him to see how he got things done. I liked the idea of travel and took over from him. Probably the best move I ever made.'

'It must be interesting work.'

'It is. But it can also be dangerous. I've been attacked quite a few times.'

'Like how?'

'With guns or knives or fists. People just don't want to be picked up and taken to prison. Understandable.'

'I can imagine,' Jason said.

'It has its compensations though. I get very well paid.'

Jason nodded. He would like to know how much Lance got paid but didn't want to ask. He could ask Gill later. He looked down at his hand and said, 'You know this is the second time my hand has been broken by a criminal. I'm getting seriously pissed off with it.'

'Tell me more,' Lance said.

Jason told him the story of Phil Gator and the attack in Woodvale. He could see that Lance was shocked, especially with all the murders that Gator did along the way.

'Sounds like another article for you to write,' Lance said to Gill.

'It certainly does,' Gill said. 'How come you never told me about this before?'

'I don't tell everyone,' Jason said. 'I keep it close to my chest.'

Then he told them the Teddy Peppers story as well. When he was finished Gill said, 'I definitely want to write this up. It's a great story.'

'The policeman involved already wrote it up for a newspaper. He called the article *Tour de Force*.'

'Nothing like a good pun,' Gill said.

Jason said, 'Maybe when Sara Shriver's new CD comes out you can do it then. I'm going to have a few songs on there and a little extra publicity wouldn't hurt.'

'Sara Shriver the actress?' Lance asked.

'Yes, she's also a country singer. She's already done one CD. She lives in London about five minutes from where I live. I befriended her and persuaded her to do some of my songs.'

'Interesting,' Lance said. He looked at Gill. 'And there's your third story. Jason and Sara Shriver.'

Gill nodded, 'You should be my agent. You two make my life look pretty boring. I really must get out of bar work.'

'Write a few more articles,' Lance said, 'and you'll be on your way. I hear the money's good.'

'The money's good but it's so hard to get anything published,' Gill said. 'It's a hand to mouth existence, so people keep telling me.'

'You can do it,' Lance said. 'I have faith in you.'

Jason looked at the two of them and wondered if they were sleeping together. Probably not. Lance would be in his fifties, probably older than him, and he couldn't imagine Gill falling for him. Besides,

Lance was probably married. Not that that meant too much these days.

'So,' Jason said to Lance. 'When you do what you have to do to Jamie Swell, will you get away with it? What if the police come looking for you afterwards?'

'I won't be doing anything worth getting caught for,' Lance said. 'And I'll be gone before you can say Hannibal Lecter.'

'That's good. But is it worth the risk?'

'Minimal risk,' Lance said. 'I know how to disappear quickly. And can you really trust the British legal system? He'll probably just get a fine and a hundred hours of community service. That won't be enough to deter him in the future.'

Jason had to agree with that; Jamie probably would get away with it. 'Well, I wish you luck.' Then Jason thought of something else. 'Is there any chance you could get my Martin guitar back for me? He nicked it when he attacked me and it's worth two grand. I've had it for about thirty years and it would mean the world to me.'

'What does it look like?'

'Just a sturdy brown guitar with Martin written on the end. He has two guitars. The other is crimson. He probably stole that one too.'

'I'll have a look, definitely,' Lance said. 'If I find it I'll leave it at Kings Cross station in one of the storage places. I'll give Gill the details. Then you can pick it up.'

'Great,' Jason said. He was beginning to like Lance more by the minute. 'I'd love to know what you're going to do to him. Just so I can gloat a little.'

Lance smiled. 'My name is Lance and I leave it to chance. That's a little saying I made up. I'll just see what happens. I wing it.'

'You wing it and then bring it,' Jason said. 'There must be a song in this somewhere.'

'I wing it and bring it and you sing it,' Lance said. Then took a sip of beer.

'I think you're both mad,' Gill said.

After one drink they left the house and walked down to The Crow's Nest where Mary Ann was working. Jason felt good walking in next to Lance the tough guy bounty hunter. Then realised that to Mary Ann, Lance would just look like some slightly overweight, middle-aged man. She seemed glad to see him though and asked about his hand. He told her he'd been attacked in his own home and she looked at him warily and went off to serve someone.

Lance ordered a bottle of beer, and bought Jason a pint. They sat down in a corner while Gill remained at the bar for a while. The sun shone through the window and for some reason Jason felt optimistic. He wondered how long that feeling would last.

\*\*\*

Ray Lane arrived at Redgate station at six thirty after he'd finished work. Jamie was waiting for him in the car park in Daisy's Polo.

Jamie hadn't spoken much to Ray since they'd been charged for molesting the barmaid. He'd been trying to avoid him and getting into more trouble, but now he needed Ray for this new task and he was sure he would rise to the occasion. He told Ray what they had to do as they drove back to Daisy's place.

'Great!' Ray said. 'That sounds like an adventure.'

Jamie couldn't believe the guy. Ray really did need his head examining. Maybe he could just push him into the quarry as well and get him out of his life for good.

Back at the house he introduced him to Daisy and Ray gave her a lustful once over. Jamie couldn't blame him really. Daisy was looking better by the hour, as if the death of the two men closest to her was doing her the world of good. Another week of this and she'd be looking like Miss World. Jamie showed Ray the body of his dad and then they went to the kitchen.

Daisy had cooked some pasta and sauce so they sat down at the small table to eat. There was a bottle of red wine there too which didn't last long with Ray around. He had three glasses while Jamie and Daisy had the rest. For dessert Daisy got out the Bakewell Tart again and made a cup of tea.

There was nowhere else to sit in the flat as the body of Glenn was in the living room. When supper was finished Jamie said he'd wrap the body up and then they could move it downstairs to the hallway. So he went to work on his dad, trying to do a decent and neat job with sheets and blankets as if that would make some kind of difference and add dignity to the situation. He breathed through his mouth as there was now a strange smell in the room. Maybe his dad had emptied his bowels. He kissed his father goodbye on the forehead before covering up his face. It took him twenty minutes to finish the job and then Ray helped him carry the mummified body to the bottom of the stairs.

Back in the living room, after Daisy had sprayed it with air freshener, they sat down in front of the TV and watched early evening rubbish with Ray making wisecracks, trying to make Daisy laugh. And he succeeded. Daisy actually laughed. Jamie just couldn't work the woman out. Maybe she was a sociopath or a black widow spider. She was definitely a widow, that was for sure.

Time passed slowly, and at half past midnight Jamie said it was time to make a move. He checked that the road was quiet, then he and Ray lifted his father out into the street and on to the back seat of the Polo. Jamie had found some large wire cutters in the flat. He was hoping he could cut through the Fuller's Earth fence this time rather than having to lift his dad over it.

They drove in silence, still quite a few cars on the road as they made the short drive. Outside the old factory Jamie turned off the main road and shut off the Polo's lights. He stopped the car at the fence and climbed out with the wire cutters.

The chain holding the gate shut looked far too thick for wire cutters though. A blow torch would have been handy. Ray came up beside him and said, 'You'll never cut that. No way in hell.'

Jamie had to agree. 'Bollocks. We'll have to lift the body over.' He almost said 'again', but stopped himself in time. Ray didn't know about the dispatching of Vernon. There was no way Jamie would tell him such a big secret and he'd told Daisy not to mention Vernon as well. So once again he pulled the car sideways to the fence and they went about the task of lifting his father's body over then dropping it on to the other side. Jamie didn't like doing that bit at all, his father hitting the ground with a heavy thud. They clambered over and stood next to the body and Ray said, 'What now?'

Jamie thought about the wheelbarrow which was now lying at the bottom of the quarry. 'We've got to get his body all the way to the quarry,' he said. 'We need something to transport him in.'

'How far is the quarry?' Ray asked.

'A good fifteen minute walk.'

Ray looked at him suspiciously. 'How come you know the area so well?'

'My dad brought me here once,' Jamie said, which wasn't a lie. 'He used to work here. Wanted to show me the layout of the area.'

Ray nodded, satisfied with the explanation. 'Why don't we just leave him in one of these buildings? No one's going to come here.'

Jamie had to agree with that. Who would come here? He looked over at the old canteen building. They could just break in there and put his father's body in the kitchen. That would be better than chucking it down into the quarry. And it would save time and effort too.

So they carried the body over to the canteen and set it on the ground outside the front door.

'Now we just have to find a way in,' Jamie said.

'Leave that to me,' Ray said. 'I'm a master at breaking and entering.'

Jamie watched as Ray walked off looking for somewhere to get in. He looked up at the stars and hoped that God, if he existed, wasn't looking down at him right then.

## CHAPTER TWENTY-THREE.

Jamie and Ray stayed the night at Daisy's, Jamie sleeping upstairs in his dad's room while Ray took the living room sofa, moaning a bit beforehand because there'd been a dead body on it a few hours previously, and that maybe some of the death spirits had seeped down into the cushions. Jamie just laughed at him while Daisy disappeared to her own room.

Jamie woke up early at seven, the sun coming through the window. He went next door for a piss, then back to his dad's room to see if there was anything he could take as a memento. He couldn't believe how few possessions his father had though. What on earth could he take? His toothbrush? In the end he settled for an old watch that was sitting on the table. It was gold in colour with a brown strap. He didn't recognise it and wondered if it was a leftover from one of his many jewellery store robberies. Probably. He took it anyway.

Downstairs he found Ray in the living room sitting in Daisy's armchair.

'Fucking awful night's sleep,' Ray said. 'I kept dreaming there was a dead man watching over me. No way am I going to work.'

'Sorry to hear that,' Jamie said. 'You can crash at my place if you like. Save you going all the way home.'

'I might just do that. What's for breakfast?'

They went to the kitchen and rustled up some tea and toast.

Ray said, 'When we're finished, let's just get the fuck out of here. This place is giving me the creeps.'

'Okay. No need to say goodbye to Daisy.'

'Did you fuck her yet?' Ray whispered.

'No,' Jamie said. 'But she's looking better everyday.'

'Maybe we could bang her before we go.'

'No, we're in enough trouble already.'

Half an hour later and they were sneaking out of the building, then making the walk towards the station.

'I'll just go straight to work,' Jamie said. 'I'll give you my flat keys and you can have a kip. I'll meet you there after work.'

'Sounds perfect,' Ray said. 'You got any porn I can watch?'

\*\*\*

Lance Boyle stayed the whole night in Jamie Swell's Camden flat, sitting in an armchair waiting for him to come home. It was a one bedroom council flat up on the third floor of a non-descript block, and the front door hadn't posed too many problems. Boyle had broken into many properties over the years, especially when he was a policeman. He'd arrived at seven last night, pulling his suitcase on wheels behind him. After a little chat with Swell he'd intended to stay in a local hotel and then catch the Eurostar to France. But Swell hadn't turned up, so Boyle had decided to stay anyway. He'd slept in armchairs before and it was cheaper than a hotel.

Now he was wondering whether to stay or go. It was none of his business really, this Gill and Jason affair. He was only doing it to impress Gill, show her what a tough guy he was. Maybe he could get her into bed one day. She was certainly built for lovin'.

The waiting reminded him of his job; travelling to houses or apartments in the middle of the night, surprising criminals with his sudden presence. Except Swell had surprised *him* by not turning up. He wondered where he was. Out clubbing? Yeah, clubbing someone over the head.

Boyle got up from the armchair at seven a.m. Went to the bathroom for a piss and to splash some water on his face. Then he walked around looking at Swell's personal possessions. There weren't many of them, not even a photo of him. Kids these days didn't need much stuff, what with downloading from the Internet. They kept everything they needed on their phone, their iPad, their tablet, or whatever. Boyle didn't have that many possessions either, seeing as how he was always on the move. He liked the nomadic life and living in hotels. It was like being a star in his own movie. Like a private eye or a hit man. Being a bounty hunter was definitely a cool way to live.

Then he remembered Jason's guitar. There were two in the living room, just as Jason had said. He unzipped the case of one of them and there it was, a brown Martin. Nice looking guitar. Boyle zipped the case up and carried it to the front door so he wouldn't forget it on his way out. Then he had a look at the other guitar. It was crimson and cheap looking, a girl's guitar. Maybe he could take that with him too. His daughter Sofia had expressed interest in learning the guitar and it would be a nice surprise present for her on his return. Perks of the job and all that. He carried it to the front door as well.

He'd give it a few more hours, see if Swell turned up, then head for Kings Cross St Pancreas and the train. Maybe Swell would return before going to work. He worked in Camden apparently, some kind of goods store that Boyle had never heard of. Fargos was it? He fixed himself some tea and toast in the kitchen and turned on the radio. He listened to the news as he ate, not much of it making any sense, though he was better travelled than most Americans and knew the layout of the world.

He was back in the living room at nine a.m. reading an old newspaper when he heard a key in the front door. He sat there and waited, tensing a little, hoping this Jamie guy wasn't too aggressive.

But the man who came in was red faced, overweight and soft looking, and looked around the hallway as if he didn't live there. Then he came into the living room, saw Boyle straightaway and said, 'Who the fuck are you?'

'I'm your worst nightmare,' Boyle said, not liking the no-respect attitude of the man. 'Who are you?'

'I'm a friend of Jamie's,' the man said. 'He gave me his keys for the day.'

'Would you happen to be Ray Lane?'

The man looked at him with surprise, amazed that Boyle should know his name.

'Who wants to know?' Lane said.

Boyle got up from the armchair, walked over to Lane and punched him on the forehead with a blow as quick and hard as a jackhammer. Lane fell to the floor at his feet like a sack of cement.

\*\*\*

When Ray Lane woke up he was tied to a chair in the middle of the small living room. Boyle was sitting there watching him, drinking a cup of tea.

Lane struggled at his arms which were tied behind his back with thin industrial black plastic straps. Boyle always carried a few around with him. They were light and unbreakable and you never knew when they'd come in handy.

'What the fuck is this?' Lane said angrily. 'And who the fuck are you exactly?'

'I'm a bounty hunter,' Boyle said. 'And you don't need to know my name.'

'A bounty hunter? I thought they went out with the western.'

'There's still a few of us around.'

'A bounty hunter,' Lane laughed. 'Why don't you go to the sweet shop then?'

Boyle smiled. 'That's quite a good joke. Can I use it for myself?'

'Do what the fuck you like. Fucking Yank.'

Boyle stood up and walked over to Lane. 'I'm here because you assaulted a friend of mine, a barmaid in Islington. Remember?'

Lane smiled up at him. 'Yeah I remember. The one with the nice tits.'

Boyle kicked him hard in the chest with the heel of his right boot and Lane yelped in pain, then toppled over backwards on to the floor, lying there unable to move. Boyle walked around behind him and put his heel on Lane's forehead.

'I don't know whether to just crush your skull right now or torture you a bit first,' he said.

'Torture me a bit first,' Lane said. 'If you please.'

Boyle had to admire the gall of the guy. He left him there and went to the kitchen. In one of the cupboards he found a toolbox and rummaged through it. Guys always kept toolboxes, that's why they were guys. He found a pair of wire clippers and took them back to the living room. Lane saw them in his hand as he entered and flinched.

'Great,' Lane said. 'Are you going to cut my balls off?'

'Wouldn't want to touch them,' Boyle said. Then knelt down beside Lane and grabbed his right ear. He snipped into it quickly, a cut of just under an inch.

Lane screamed, a piercing sound like that of an electrocuted pig. Boyle watched him bleeding on to the grey carpet, fear now etched on the fat man's face. At last he had his attention.

'I just want to warn you and your friend Jamie,' Boyle said. 'Never to do anything like that again. And when you go to court you'll plead guilty and take your punishment. If I hear your name again in a negative context I'll be back to do your other ear. And *then* I'll cut your balls off.'

Lane looked at him through eyes of pain. The blood was squirting out but it wouldn't kill him. Boyle went to the bathroom and grabbed a towel from the rack. Went back to Lane and jammed it next to his head on the floor. The towel would soak up the blood for a while and it would eventually stop.

'And give that message to your friend Swell too,' Boyle said. 'I want you both to stop fucking around and live like decent human beings. Or you'll both end up in jail. And what's the point of that? Life is for the living, not for the wasting.'

Lane looked at him with a puzzled expression. Boyle felt like he was giving a lecture to one of his younger delinquents. 'Where is Swell right now?'

'At work you fucker,' Lane said.

Boyle knelt down beside Lane and searched his pockets, found his smart phone and stood back up. He found Swell's number with no problems and rang it. It went straight to voice mail so Boyle said, 'Your friend Ray Lane is in a spot of bother. He's bleeding on your living room floor, so when you get the chance you'd better come home and call an ambulance.' Then he hung up. 'No answer. Your friend isn't there in your time of need.'

'That's because he works in a fucking basement,' Lane said.

'Well, that's tough luck for you. Hopefully he'll go out for lunch and check his messages. I'll leave the door on the latch. Maybe the postman will find you instead.'

Then Boyle walked into the front hall, picked up his suitcase and the two guitars and left.

It took him twenty minutes to walk to Kings Cross, his suitcase trundling along behind him with one guitar lying on top of it and the other slung over his shoulder.

It was good to be out in the fresh air after being stuck in the small flat. It was a shame Jamie Swell hadn't come home but Ray Lane would pass on the message. Sometimes you just had to scare people to get them to do what you wanted. It wasn't rocket science, just common sense.

He looked at his watch. It wasn't even ten yet. Plenty of time to make the train and have a good look around the new station they'd built. That's what he liked about travelling; it broadened your outlook. He'd also drop off the Martin guitar somewhere and ring Gill to tell her how to pick it up.

Boyle thought about his next pick-up, a twenty-five year old guy called Pearson, living in a Paris suburb. He hadn't been to the city of romance for a few years. He was looking forward to it. Get some decent coffee, maybe watch a subtitled film. Then get down to business.

## CHAPTER TWENTY-FOUR.

Two days after being attacked, Jason carried on with his lessons. His pupils were sympathetic to the fact that he could no longer play, and that he would have to instruct them with words instead, a bit of a challenge but doable. At least he could show them chords with his left hand, while his right hand lay limp over the edge of his guitar. He also had to accept the fact that some of his students would disappear for a few months, waiting for him to heal, and that some of them wouldn't return later. Such was life. He had enough money to get him through his convalescence. Just. And he would see if the council could help him out as well, though he wasn't holding his breath on that front.

Sara and Rick came round to see him a week after his attack. They sat in his living room and told him that they wanted to use three of his songs on their next CD: 'Whisky Lingers', 'One Guitar', and 'Life is a Road'.

'Fantastic,' Jason said. 'That should pay a few bills.'

Rick had recovered from the blow to his head and was back at Sara's house regularly, practising and other stuff. Jason wondered what the 'other stuff' was. Were they having an affair?

'If your hand is healed in time,' Rick said, 'we'd like you to play and sing on our CD. If your hand isn't okay then you could just sing.'

'That would be great,' Jason said. 'Something to look forward to.'

'And when we go out touring,' Sara said, 'perhaps you'd like to come with us? The money won't be great, but it'll be better than teaching. And I pay for all the accommodation. It'll be a small adventure.'

'Excellent,' Jason said. 'Count me in.'

'So you'd better learn all our songs, old and new.' She opened her handbag and took out a large brown envelope. 'Here's a copy of my CD and some lyric and chord sheets. They're not difficult to learn.' She laid the envelope on the settee.

'My homework,' Jason said. 'I'll do the best I can with one hand.'

'Said the actress to the bishop,' Rick said.

'And how have you recovered?' Jason asked Sara. 'I never did learn the details of your ordeal. What happened exactly?'

'The two men came into my house and I found them in the music room. They attacked me and then tried to feel me up. I hit the eldest one over the head with a microphone stand and they fled. They also attacked Rick, knocking him out cold.'

'Jesus. What a pair of arseholes.'

'I was just wondering,' Sara said. 'Maybe the two men who attacked me were the same two who attacked you?'

Jason could feel himself blushing. 'I doubt it. Is that what the police told you?'

'No, I haven't asked them. I've only seen them once since. They'll probably forget all about it and the two men will never be caught.'

Jason nodded. 'More than likely.'

Gill had told him that Lance Boyle had been to Jamie Swell's flat but had ended up attacking the wrong man, his friend Ray Lane. So Jamie had got away with it once again. At least Jason had his Martin guitar back though. That was one thing he could thank Lance for. He'd left it at Kings Cross station and Jason had picked it up.

The front doorbell rang. Jason excused himself and went out into the hallway. When he opened the door Jamie Swell was standing there. Jason was shocked and a little worried.

'I want my guitar back,' Jamie said. Getting straight to the point, not so much as a hello.

Jason didn't know what he was talking about. 'What guitar? The one you stole from me?'

'No, my red one,' Jamie said. 'Your bounty hunter friend took them both. I presume he gave them to you.'

Jason shook his head. 'I got my Martin back. I don't know what happened to the other one. I know nothing about it.'

'Fucking liar,' Jamie said, and pushed past him into the hallway.

Before Jason could stop him, Jamie was walking straight into his flat where he was confronted by the sight of Sara and Rick, sitting there looking at him with puzzled expressions.

Sara stood up and said, 'What the hell are you doing here?' She turned to Rick and said, 'This is one of my attackers.'

Rick stood up with an angry look on his face. He'd been knocked out so quickly a week ago that he hadn't had time to look at his assailants. 'Is that right?' he said.

Jamie said, 'I've come to get my guitar back.' He looked around the room with a worried expression on his face.

Jason said, 'You won't find it here. I haven't got it.'

'Give me another one then,' Jamie said.

'*I'll* give you another one,' Rick said, and quick as a flash he was tussling with Jamie and trying to get an arm lock on him. Jason shut the door so Jamie couldn't escape.

Jamie didn't like being touched by Rick and a torrent of abuse came from his mouth. Sara and Jason stood back to watch. Eventually Rick got Jamie around the neck and dragged him towards a chair.

'Call the police,' he said to Sara. 'We're going to make a citizen's arrest.'

Jason was amazed by Rick's strength, then remembered that he'd once been in the army and was also a personal trainer. Jamie couldn't release himself from his grip. Rick told Jason to get some guitar leads and the two of them tied Jamie into a chair, the same chair that Jamie and his dad had tied him into. When that was done they stood back to survey their handiwork.

'The police are on their way,' Sara said. 'Nice job.' Then she looked at Jason and said, 'How does this guy know you?'

Jason could feel himself blushing again. 'It's a long story,' he said.

Sara said, 'I think you've got some explaining to do.'

\*\*\*

Daisy carried the last of her things down to the Polo then walked along the street to her landlord's place and dropped two envelopes through the letterbox. One of them held two weeks rent for Glenn's flat and the other held two weeks rent for her flat. That would give her plenty of time to disappear, get herself out of the country and into France and then Spain.

She walked back down the street and knocked on Angie's door.

'Hi gorgeous,' Angie said, letting her into the house with a big smile.

Daisy kissed her on the lips and they had a warm hug. 'I'm ready to go,' Daisy said. 'All packed and loaded and the landlord hoodwinked.'

'I'll get you the keys,' Angie said.

Daisy walked into the living room and sat down on the sofa. She'd been Angie's lover for nearly a year, and now she was disappearing to Angie's flat in Spain. Angie would sell her house in the next few months and then join her. Their meticulous plan had worked better than expected, and Daisy had Vernon's lifetime savings to live on as well. She could always get a job in Spain eventually. She'd secretly been learning Spanish while Vernon was at work.

Angie came back in and sat down beside her. She handed over the keys to her Spanish home.

'I'll miss you,' she said.

'Me too,' Daisy said. 'But soon we'll be together for good. And we can always Skype.'

'Can't wait for that. No more Redgate and no more men.'

'Poor Glenn,' Daisy said. 'He was quite taken with you.'

'I could tell. He had the vanity of all men. Thinking that every woman fancies them.'

Daisy nodded. 'Shall we have a quick one before I go?'

Angie shook her head. 'I'm still recovering from last night. And still a bit sore.'

'Okay. I did get carried away a bit.'

They stood up and had a final kiss and hug in the hallway.

'I'll see you soon,' Angie said, and Daisy walked out and over to her car. She climbed in and drove slowly away from the rotting damp house of Frenches Road and the nightmare of violent Vernon and gloomy Glenn. She hoped they were both rotting in hell - wherever they were buried.

## *CHAPTER TWENTY-FIVE.*

Down in the Argos storeroom, Jamie Swell was feeling a little stressed. A large delivery of boxes had just come in and they were short staffed. He was working at twice the speed of sound trying to get things out of boxes and on to shelves. Meanwhile, Siva the manager, was no doubt sitting up in his office drinking a cup of tea and thinking about Manchester United his favourite football team. When he could really be down here, helping him out.

It was two days since he'd walked into Jason's flat to try and get his guitar back, a plan that would have worked had Sara Shriver not been there with that other guy, the one called Rick. He'd found out later from the police that Rick had once been in the army, which was double bad luck. How the fuck was he meant to fight off an ex marine? The man had arms of steel.

The police had taken him to Chiswick police station where he'd been charged for the attack on Sara and also for breaking Jason's finger. They'd also asked him about his dad's whereabouts, so Jamie had told them that he was living down in Redgate in a house in Frenches Road. He wondered how Daisy would explain that one away when they arrived on her doorstep. Probably just play dumb and his dad would go down as a missing person. So now Jamie had three charges against him, and he was going to prison no doubt about it - when they eventually got around to seeing him in court.

It had been a week or so since Ray had been attacked in Jamie's flat. Jamie had found the message from the bounty hunter on his phone at lunchtime and hurried back to the flat to find Ray on the floor in a pool of blood, looking a bit pale and almost unconscious. Jamie had cut the plastic straps from his wrists and taken him to the bathroom to clean him up. Then Ray had taken a long hot bath, lying there in pink water when his ear started bleeding again. And he hadn't even cleaned the bath afterwards, leaving a pink rim around the edge for Jamie to clean off. Jamie had eventually persuaded him to go to hospital. There was one just down the road, a ten minute walk. So Ray had wandered off feeling sorry for himself, holding a large wad of toilet paper against his ear, and Jamie had returned to Argos. It was only later that he'd noticed that both of his guitars were missing.

So then he'd planned his little visit to Jason's. What a big mistake that was in hindsight. All for the sake of a red guitar. A guitar he didn't really want to play anyway, it was the principal of the matter.

He hadn't seen Ray since. No big loss. Ray hadn't known who the bounty hunter was, some big fucking American, but he'd passed on his message. Don't fuck around anymore was basically it. Which Jamie had ignored straight away. He didn't listen to dumb Americans, especially ones who threatened him.

Jamie missed his dad. He'd never thought he'd miss him so much. After the bounty hunter incident he'd even picked up his mobile to ring him then realised that his dad was in fact dead, lying in his cocoon of sheets and blankets in the canteen of Fuller's Earth. For a few seconds Jamie had even thought of catching the train down there to visit his old man, sit next to his rotting corpse and have a few words. Then he realised that no, that wasn't such a smart idea, the smell would be too bad. So he'd slumped on his sofa and had a delayed reaction cry, feeling sorry for himself and his dear departed dad. Now he was truly alone in the world, except for his mum up near Newcastle. And he sure as hell didn't want to see her anymore.

His only friend in the world was Ray really, and he wasn't much of a friend, getting him into trouble all the time. All these thoughts came flooding back as he toiled away in the Argos storeroom, fighting the never ending tide of boxes coming in.

Eventually he'd had enough. He picked up the internal phone and rang upstairs to the office where Siva picked up.

'I really need some help down here,' Jamie said. 'I'm struggling under a tsunami of boxes.'

Much to his surprise Siva said, 'Okay, I'll be down in a minute.'

Jamie put the phone down and took a few deep breaths. Siva was coming to help him. Well glory be. Maybe Siva could be his new friend. Then he thought, fuck that, he'd just want to talk about football all the time.

Jamie picked up his Stanley knife and carried on slicing boxes open. What was the point in getting a new friend anyway? In a few months he'd be locked up somewhere doing time. Like father like son.

\*\*\*

Jason was lying on his sofa feeling sorry for himself. It was several days since the arrest of Jamie Swell in his flat. After the police had taken him away, Jason had explained to Sara and Rick his connection with Jamie, and Sara had decided that she couldn't work with a person who had sent two criminals to her house. She was a famous person after all, and the people she worked with had to be trusted. She just couldn't understand why Jason had given Jamie and his dad her house number. What was he thinking?

Later, Jason had once again castigated himself for being so honest. He could have said that he'd pointed Sara's house out to Jamie when they'd walked past it the one time he'd given Jamie a lesson. That wouldn't have seemed so bad. But it was too late now. And then yesterday Rick had rung to tell him, after a considerable amount of thought, that they no longer required his songs on their CD either. They were cutting him right out of their lives. He cursed his never ending bad luck, his life as a failure. It was all turning to shit once again.

The front doorbell rang.

Jason climbed nervously off the sofa and went to answer it. He wondered if it was Jamie Swell again, come to get his guitar back for a second time. Nothing would surprise him anymore. But when he opened the door he was amazed to find Gill standing there.

'Hi,' she said. 'I was hoping you were home.'

Jason couldn't believe what he was seeing, in fact he hadn't even known that she had his address. 'What's up?' he asked. 'More trouble?'

Gill shook her head. 'Are you going to invite me in?'

'Sure,' Jason said, and stood back to let her inside.

When they were in his flat he said to her, 'How do you know where I live? Did I tell you once?'

'You gave me your card once,' Gill said. 'When we first met. Trying to impress me.'

Jason remembered now. That was quite a while ago. He was amazed that Gill had kept the card. Then she reached into her large shoulder bag and brought out a bottle of champagne.

'I thought we'd celebrate,' she said. 'My article on Lance Boyle has been accepted and will be published in a few months. I've also received a very large cheque.'

'That's great,' Jason said. 'Well done. Some good news at last.'

'And we can also celebrate the fact that Jamie Swell is out of our lives. He'll be going to prison now, that's for sure.'

'Yeah,' Jason said. 'The best place for him.'

He led Gill into the kitchen and took two champagne glasses from a cupboard. He took the cold bottle from her then realised he wouldn't be able to get the cork out with one hand so handed it back. As Gill worked on the cork, he told her his bad news about Sara Shriver and the CD that would never happen. The cork popped out of the bottle and hit the ceiling.

'That's a real shame,' Gill said, pouring into the glasses. 'I thought that things were finally happening for you.'

'So did I. But it seems they're happening to you instead. And how is Lance?'

'He's fine. He's back in the States. Picked up a teenager from Paris and returned with him.'

'Is he your new boyfriend?'

Gill laughed. 'No way. Do you really think I'd want to go out with a bounty hunter?'

'I thought there was something between you two?'

'I think *he* would like something between us two. Like his big redneck friend.'

Jason didn't understand. 'Redneck friend? You'll have to explain that one.'

Gill shook her head. 'And you being such a big Jackson Browne fan.'

'I still don't know what you're talking about.'

Gill handed him a glass and they chinked them together. 'You know that song of his called 'Redneck Friend'?'

Jason nodded.

'What do you think the 'Redneck Friend' is?'

Jason shrugged. 'A redneck friend?'

'It's his penis,' Gill said. 'And I quote, "Honey let me introduce you to my Redneck Friend". He's talking about his prick.'

'Ah,' Jason said. 'I didn't know that.'

'So no, Lance and I aren't an item, though I think he would like his Redneck Friend and me to become acquainted.'

'I get it now.' Jason smiled. He had never heard Gill talk dirty before. He quite liked it.

'And how about yours?' Gill asked. 'Would your Redneck Friend like to be introduced to me?'

Jason felt his face going red. 'I'm sure he would,' he said. 'But I've only got one hand to work with.'

'Don't worry about that,' Gill said. 'I've got two.'

***THE END***

Jerry Raine is the author of ten crime novels all available on Kindle. They are, in order of publication: *Smalltime, Frankie Bosser Comes Home, Slaphead Chameleon, Small Change, Some Like It Cold, Camden Calling, Missing In Acton, Shilo, No Company Allowed,* and *Cowboy Dreams.*

Jerry currently lives in London where he plays guitar and writes songs, and occasionally performs. In the past he has been a support act for Christy Moore, Steve Forbert, and Gretchen Peters. He also did a UK and Ireland tour with US country singer Iris DeMent in 1998. A selection of his songs can be found on the SoundCloud website.

All song lyrics in this book were written by Jerry Raine – except where stated.

Printed in Great Britain
by Amazon.co.uk, Ltd.,
Marston Gate.